You're invited to a

CREEPOVER ™

Off the Wall

written by P. J. Night

SIMON SPOTLIGHT
New York   London   Toronto   Sydney   New Delhi

SIMON SPOTLIGHT
An imprint of Simon & Schuster Children's Publishing Division
1230 Avenue of the Americas, New York, New York 10020
© 2013 by Simon & Schuster, Inc.
All rights reserved, including the right of reproduction in whole or in part in any form.
SIMON SPOTLIGHT and colophon are registered trademarks of Simon & Schuster, Inc.
YOU'RE INVITED TO A CREEPOVER is a trademark of Simon & Schuster, Inc.
Text by Ann Hodgman
For information about special discounts for bulk purchases, please contact Simon & Schuster Special Sales at 1-866-506-1949 or business@simonandschuster.com.
Manufactured in the United States of America 0513 OFF
First Edition 10 9 8 7 6 5 4 3 2 1
ISBN 978-1-4424-7238-9
ISBN 978-1-4424-7239-6 (eBook)
Library of Congress Catalog Card Number 2012950418

PROLOGUE

For centuries the girl had been asleep.

Asleep, tightly wrapped, in her close-fitting bed. Asleep, undisturbed, under tons of silent sand.

Asleep through turmoil and wars and famines on the Earth's surface. Asleep when the mighty Nile flooded its banks, and asleep when decades of drought wiped out whole villages.

Civilizations had come and gone while she slept, and nothing had disturbed her dreamless sleep. She had slept through the early days of her tomb's discovery. Through years of patient, careful digging as the sand above her was brushed away. She had slept as her sarcophagus was lifted into the glaring sunlight of an

Egyptian day and carried away from its resting place.

And for the next hundred years she had slept in a dusty office in an Egyptian museum, visited by almost no one.

But now, in the darkness, she began to stir. Something was coming through to her. Sounds. Movement. Then the sense that she was in the wrong place. It was time to wake up.

In the darkness, the girl frowned.

CHAPTER 1

"I don't want to go," Jane whispered to herself. "*I don't want to go.*"

Ahead of her the huge, cavernous lobby of the Templeton Memorial Museum was ringing with the clamor of fifty other girls Jane's age. They were lined up in front of a long table, eagerly signing in for the Templeton Lock-In.

A poster on the wall above the tables blasted the neon-pink words: THRILL TO AN OVERNIGHT EXPERIENCE BEHIND THE SCENES OF THE MUSEUM! But from her place at the end of the line, Jane was not thrilled. Not at all. Not one bit.

"It will be good for you," her mother had said to her

that morning. "You need to socialize with more girls your own age."

But what, Jane wondered, *am I supposed to say to girls I've never seen before in my life? And how on Earth can I possibly spend an entire sleepover with them?*

She cast a miserable glance around the lobby—a bustling hive of girls and their parents and all their random good-bye conversations.

"Dad, I don't *need* an alarm clock! They'll wake us up, I swear!" And "I don't see your allergy pillow, honey. Where's your allergy pillow?" And *"Fine,* then! I don't want to hear another word about it!" And "No, Mommy, don't hug me. Everyone will think I'm a baby."

I'm just not anything like these girls, Jane thought. *I can tell just by looking at them. Why, why did I have to—*

"Are you here to register, dear?" came the friendly voice of a woman in front of her.

Jane jumped out of her thoughts. The line had been moving along without her noticing, and now she was standing right at the registration table.

"I guess so," said Jane. Nervously she twisted a hank of her blond hair around one finger.

"Okay! What's your name?"

"Jane Meunier."

The woman glanced through a sheaf of papers and checked off Jane's name. "Have you done a lock-in with us before, Jane?"

"No. We—I—uh—just moved here," Jane stammered. "I don't know anything about *anything*."

The woman chuckled. "Well, then, you are in for a wonderful surprise. This is going to be the best night of your life! Now, where's your sleeping bag?"

Jane pointed to a pile of blankets in her basket.

"Oh, no sleeping bag?" remarked the woman. "Did you bring a foam pad to put under your blankets? That floor can feel awfully hard."

"Foam pad?" exclaimed Jane. "I've never heard of using a foam pad! Oh, I *knew* something was going to go wrong right away!"

"Don't look so worried!" said the woman. "They've got extra foam mattresses in the Great Hall for people who need them. And you'll have a wonderful time. The lock-in is one of our most popular events. There's a huge waiting list every time."

"She's right. The lock-in is really, really fun." This voice was coming from behind Jane. She turned around to see a

5

girl—who had dark hair and brown eyes—smiling at her. "I'm so excited!" the girl continued. "I've been waiting to be old enough ever since my sister did a lock-in here three years ago. Hi, Mrs. Crawford," she added. "I guess you know I'm here to register for the lock-in tonight."

"Yes indeedy, Lucy," said the woman at the table. "I've got your paperwork right here! Jane, this is Lucy Nasim. Lucy has attended every single Templeton Museum event in the history of the world."

"That's pretty much true," said Lucy. "Pottery workshops, plant hunts in the park, Meet the Owls—you name it. I *love* this museum. I totally wish I *lived* here."

Jane smiled shyly at Lucy. At this moment, she wasn't exactly feeling the same way, but she could already tell that Lucy was really nice.

Mrs. Crawford handed each girl a name tag. "Lucy, this is Jane's first time at the museum. Why don't you take her to the Great Hall? The group leaders are already there. And help her get a foam mattress, okay?"

"Of course I will," said Lucy, shouldering her backpack.

"And Lucy—none of your practical jokes tonight, okay?" Mrs. Crawford turned to Jane and said, "Lucy can be kind of a prankster. Don't let her play any tricks."

Lucy rolled her eyes in mock exasperation. "I'll try to be good. Let's go, Jane. I know *everything* about this museum," she added with a laugh as they began walking. "The Great Hall's where we're going to be sleeping. It's down at the far end of the building. I think the museum people put it there because they like you to walk past some of their greatest hits on the way."

"Greatest hits?"

"Oh, you know, like some of the most famous stuff. There's a pearl the size of a baseball, for instance. And what some people think might have been King Arthur's crown. And in there is the Hall of Mythology," said Lucy. "It's superpopular."

Jane looked around at all the lifelike statues. Most of them were beautiful, but some were a bit creepy. Jane shuddered. In the center of the gallery, a marble boy was struggling to free himself from the tentacles of a massive marble sea serpent. Behind the sea serpent, Jane could see a wall mosaic of a ten-foot-tall woman who seemed to have snakes for hair. And next to the snake-haired woman, even taller, was a battered wooden statue of some kind of monster with not one, but three ferocious dog heads.

"Those myths can get pretty weird," Lucy said cheerfully. "But I guess people like the exhibit—it's always crowded."

It was thinning out now that the museum was about to close. People were hurrying past the girls on their way toward the lobby, and as Jane and Lucy passed the next exhibit hall, its lights blinked off. Glancing back, Jane realized that the mythology gallery was also dark now. For some reason, she didn't like the thought of that sea serpent and the snake-haired woman standing silent and motionless in a darkened room.

"Ta-da! Here's the Great Hall!" Lucy exclaimed.

The Great Hall was a huge round chamber with a vaulted ceiling so high above the girls' heads that Jane wasn't sure she could actually see the top. As they walked in, Jane noticed that the hall had four identical entryways spaced at equal intervals, like the directions on a compass. She and Lucy were passing through the south entrance. It had an old-looking map of the South Pole over the door, but that was the only thing that distinguished it from the other three entrances.

"I always go in through this door," said Lucy. "I love Antarctica."

But Jane wasn't paying attention. She was staring into the Great Hall, which was now a hive of excited girls. Some were laying out their sleeping bags and arranging pillows on top of them. Some were studying the murals lining the curved walls. Some were standing around chatting in groups of three or four. And all of them were shouting at the top of their lungs—or that's how it seemed to Jane.

"There's Lucy! *Loooocy!* LOOOOCEEEEEYYY!" someone screamed, and a girl with curly red hair and round blue eyes raced up to them.

"I was beginning to wonder when you were going to get here," the girl said, panting. She looked over at Jane. "Hey, who's this?"

"This is Jane. It's her first time here," Lucy answered. "Jane, this is Cailyn. She goes to school with me."

Cailyn tossed Jane a quick smile and instantly launched into a long description of her summer. "And then we went to the Silver Islands and I learned how to water ski and almost broke my leg, but it turned out to be a sprain, but I think a sprain hurts even more, and then I went to camp for two weeks and I got *the* most horrible sunburn you ever saw, and then my brother and

I went to my aunt's farm in Danville . . ."

"*Lucy! I've missed you so much!*" Another girl had just rushed up, and two others followed her. *Is everyone here a friend of Lucy's?* Jane wondered. Within a couple of minutes, she and Lucy were surrounded by a cluster of excited girls.

About twenty conversations seemed to be going on at once. Jane did her best to keep up. All these girls seemed pretty nice, she realized. Probably kids who *wanted* to spend a night in a museum were interesting and fun.

There was one girl in the group, Megan, who seemed to be even more nervous than Jane. "These floors are awfully slippery," she told Jane earnestly right after they'd been introduced. "We're going to have to walk *very* carefully. I made sure to wear shoes that have a lot of traction."

So yes, it was probably safe to say that Megan was scared too. Also, Jane reminded herself, she *couldn't* be the only shy person in a group of fifty girls. What about that girl hanging back at the outer edge of the group, for instance? The one with the straight dark hair and the sour expression? She looked sort of scared, sort of stuck up, and sort of, well, angry, Jane decided. But what was there to be mad about?

Abruptly the girl seemed to realize that Jane

was looking at her. She glared back at Jane, her eyes narrowed.

Jane felt bad for being rude. She gave the girl an embarrassed smile.

But the girl didn't smile back. If anything, she seemed to get even angrier.

I dare you to speak to me, her look was conveying. *I dare you.*

CHAPTER 2

Jane nudged Lucy. "Do you know that girl back there?" she whispered.

"I don't think so, but she looks lonely," Lucy remarked.

Jane was working up the courage to disagree with her new acquaintance, but before she had a chance, Lucy was calling the angry girl over. Head held high, the girl strode into the center of the group.

"My name is Daria," she said stiffly.

"Hi, Daria!" said Lucy brightly. "I'm Lucy, and this is Jane, and this is Cailyn, and this is Grace, and this is—"

"That is way too many names," Daria interrupted.

Lucy paused. "You're right," she said, smiling gamely.

"You'll learn all our names by the end of the night anyway. Why bother learning them all at once?"

Daria did not return the smile.

"So, um . . . are you from around here?" Lucy asked, trying to engage the girl.

"No," said Daria.

There was another pause.

"Well, that's—nice," Lucy said uncertainly. "Jane's new here too. Right, Jane?"

"Uh—yes. Hi, Daria, I'm Jane."

"I heard Lucy say your name. You don't have to tell it to me again," was Daria's reply.

Well, nice to meet you, too! Jane was tempted to retort sarcastically, but luckily a deep gong clanged through the Great Hall before she could. Everyone turned to see two women standing in the center of the room. One was athletic and energetic looking, with a halo of short auburn curls. The other was taller and had straight black hair that fell to her waist in a shining sheet.

"Could everyone come here and sit down?" the auburn-haired woman called.

Without a word, Daria turned her back on Jane and Lucy and walked toward the two women.

"Ugh, she is *awful!*" Jane whispered to Lucy as they crossed the room after her.

"Maybe she's just shy," Lucy murmured back. "Let's give her a chance."

But Jane knew what shy looked like, and she was pretty sure that shyness wasn't Daria's problem. *More like stuck-up,* she thought.

When the girls were all assembled, the leaders introduced themselves.

"Hello. I'm Willow."

"And I'm Katherine," said the woman with long black hair. "Willow and I are college students in art history, and we're going to be in charge of you guys for the night. Before we start this evening's tour, I'm going to tell you some cool stuff about the museum. Then Willow's going to give you the boring stuff about the rules. That won't be your favorite part of the night, but bear with her."

The Templeton Memorial Museum was a century old, Katherine told the girls, and it had some of the greatest collections of art, history, and science in the world. The girls at the lock-in would tour some of the most famous exhibits and get a peek behind the scenes as well. They'd be served dinner and breakfast in the museum restaurant. "They have great food," Katherine reassured everyone.

She continued, "One of the museum's trustees—a member of the Templeton family—came up with the idea for these lock-ins about ten years ago. He wanted to make the museum even more interesting for kids. We think most of the kids in the city would agree that he succeeded. The museum holds these lock-ins once a month for middle-school and high school kids, alternating between sessions for boys and girls. There's always a waiting list."

Megan, the ultranervous girl, raised her hand. "Why are they called lock-ins? It makes us sound like prisoners!"

"They're called lock-ins because . . ." Katherine dropped her voice to a hollow, mysterious moan. *"No one can get out and no one can get in."*

Megan gave a frightened gasp.

"Just for your own safety, of course," Katherine finished with a chuckle. "We don't want anyone wandering off, and we certainly don't want anyone from outside to wander into the museum."

"Wander *into* the museum?" echoed Megan in a

panicky voice. "Has that happened before? *Who* wandered in? Did any of the exhibits get stolen? Why weren't the burglar alarms working? Did anything else bad happen?"

"No one has ever wandered in," Katherine answered hastily. "That was just a figure of speech! We're going to have lots of fun tonight, but—well, I guess this is a good time for Willow to talk about the rules."

Now the auburn-haired woman stepped forward. "We're sure you're a responsible bunch," she began. "All the same, there are a few rules we must ask you to keep in mind."

"They always 'ask' you to keep rules in mind," Lucy muttered to her friends. "What they really mean is, they're telling you to obey them a hundred percent."

"The most important rule is, *don't separate from the group*. This is a big, big building, and it's very easy to get lost. Do not go *anywhere* by yourself," said Willow.

"I know this museum very well," Daria added for seemingly no reason. "I couldn't get lost."

Jane rolled her eyes. Daria probably just thought she was better than everyone else.

Willow went on as if she hadn't heard. "The other

very important rule is not to leave the Great Hall once we come back here after the tour and dinner. In other words, lights out means no leaving and wandering around. There are night guards posted throughout the museum. On lock-in nights, they help keep an eye on our guests. But as you can imagine, that's not their main job. Please obey the lights-out rule so the guards can watch the exhibits and not you!" Willow was smiling, but she sounded as if she meant it.

"What if we have to go to the bathroom in the middle of the night and everyone else is asleep?" asked Megan. That was one question Jane was glad to hear. She'd been wondering the same thing.

Katherine pointed to a far corner of the room. "There is a bathroom over there. You will all use that one."

But Megan wasn't done asking questions. "And what if there's some kind of emergency and we have to go home?"

"This is my fifth time doing this and no one has ever had to leave in the middle of the night," Katherine assured her. "But on the off chance that happens, then wake up one of us. Wake up Willow, for instance," she added, laughing.

Willow didn't seem to think that was so funny. "The point is, *no walking around the halls by yourself*," she said. "This museum has a complicated floor plan. The ground floor, especially. It's practically like a maze. So no wandering off, or you may never be seen again."

Before Megan had a chance to start worrying again, Katherine spoke up. "Willow is just joking," she said soothingly. "Don't worry, girls. We're here to look after you. We'll make sure you don't get lost."

When the leaders led the girls out of the Great Hall, Jane noticed that Megan stayed very close to Katherine.

Jane couldn't help smiling to herself. Of course she'd been a little on edge at the beginning, but it definitely made her feel better to see someone who was a hundred times more nervous than she was.

"We always begin our tour with a look at Blanche Templeton. None of us would be here if it hadn't been for her," said Willow a few minutes later.

Just beyond the lobby was a huge portrait in an ornate gilded frame. It showed a pale, sad-looking woman dressed all in black. Even the handkerchief she was clutching was black-edged. A little mahogany table stood next to her. On it were four miniature portraits with a newspaper next to them. Across the top of the newspaper was a banner headline: TITANIC SINKS ON MAIDEN VOYAGE; HUNDREDS LOST AT SEA.

"Why did the artist put in that newspaper?" asked Lucy. "It's a strange thing to have in a painting."

"Well, Mrs. Templeton and her husband, Arthur, were an important couple in the city," Willow said. "They gave money to all kinds of good causes, especially educational ones. The Templetons had three daughters. In April of 1912, Mr. Templeton brought the girls to England for a special treat—a trip on the Titanic. When the ship hit that iceberg, Mr. Templeton and the three girls lost their lives. Their bodies were never recovered."

"Is that why Mrs. Templeton looks so sad in the picture?" asked Jane.

"Exactly," said Willow. "Mrs. Templeton never got over the shock of her family's death. She dressed all in black until the end of her life. But some of her friends persuaded her that the best way to honor the memory of her husband and daughters was to make a contribution to the city in their name. She decided to donate the funds to start a world-class natural history and art museum. That's why this is called the Templeton *Memorial* Museum."

The girls stared at the portrait for a few seconds until Megan broke the silence. "I hate thinking that this *whole museum* was built to honor some dead girls. It's like we're walking on their graves!"

"I suppose that's one way to look at it," Willow said. "But this way, Blanche Templeton was able to help generations of children who came after her. Anyway, now that you know who started this museum, let's take a peek behind the scenes before dinner. We're going to show you an exhibit that won't be open to the public for another week."

"But we're allowed to go in, right?" asked Megan instantly.

Willow gave a little sigh. "Yes, Megan," she said. "We're allowed to go in."

"I don't think I want to go in," said Megan a few minutes later.

The girls and the two leaders were standing in front of a huge sign that read:

INSECTS: EARTH'S MOST SUCCESSFUL LIFE FORM

TEN QUINTILLION AND COUNTING!

(AND DON'T GET US STARTED ON THE SPIDERS.)

"In case you're wondering, ten quintillion has nineteen zeros," said Willow. "*Nineteen.* For every human being on Earth today, there are more than two hundred million insects. Of course we're not going to see *all* of them in this exhibit," she added. (A few of the girls laughed politely.) "Just some of the highlights. We're going to start with the Butterfly Pavilion."

To get into the Butterfly Pavilion, the group had to pass through two doors. The leaders wouldn't open the second door until all the girls had come through the first one. "We have to make absolutely sure that none of the butterflies escape into the main museum," said Willow. When the first door had clicked shut behind them, the girls found themselves packed into a small chamber in front of the second door.

"The Butterfly Pavilion is very warm," Katherine told them. "Butterflies and moths like it that way, but it may be a little much for some of you. You'll be more comfortable if you leave your sweaters and sweatshirts in here."

"Hurry up, though," Megan added. "Because it feels as if there's not enough air in this tiny room. I think we're using up the oxygen too fast."

Cailyn groaned. "Megan, do you really think the museum would build an exhibit that didn't have enough oxygen?"

"I know, but there are so many of us and—"

Before Megan could finish, Katherine had pulled open the heavy door into the Butterfly Pavilion. And it was so beautiful in there that even Megan stopped worrying for a while.

The first thing they noticed was that the space was filled with flowers. Dozens of different kinds bloomed along the pathways and climbed up the walls. There were flowering trees, too, and a mossy stream with a little waterfall was bubbling along through the middle of the room. And so many butterflies were flying through the air, sipping nectar from flowers and resting on branches, that Jane could hardly believe the scene was real.

"You probably already know that most butterflies and moths live on nectar," Willow explained. "That's why we have all the flowers in here. But some of them eat tree sap and pollen. Some of them eat manure—"

"*Gross!*" a girl shrieked.

"And most of them love salty minerals. Like the dissolved minerals in puddles or the salt on your skin when you sweat. Hold up a finger—like this—and see what happens!"

When the girls copied her, butterflies landed on the hands of at least half of them. One even came to rest on Lucy's nose.

"That's a tiger swallowtail," said Katherine. "Tiger swallowtails like pink flowers the best, but I guess they'll take noses when they get the chance."

"I only wish phones were allowed so I could take a picture," Lucy said to Jane a few minutes later as they wandered down one of the paths.

"I wish it was a teeny bit cooler," said Jane. "I think I'm sweaty enough to attract all the butterflies in here. Oh, hi, Daria," she added as she and Lucy turned a corner.

Daria had been bending over to examine a tiny moth inside a lily. Now she stood up slowly. She looked amazingly cool, Jane thought—not a bead of sweat anywhere. She hadn't even unzipped her sweatshirt.

"Aren't you *roasting*?" Lucy asked her.

"I like it this way," said Daria. She lifted her hand gracefully into the air. A second later, a moth Jane hadn't seen before began flapping toward them.

"Look at that moth! It's huge!" Jane said. "Daria, I think it's heading right for your hand!"

The moth did seem to be especially interested in Daria. Several other girls had noticed it by now. They were waving their own hands in the air to try to lure it over. But it kept slowly flying straight toward Daria.

Lucy called down the path to Katherine, who was showing some of the girls her insect guide. "Katherine, can you come and tell us what kind this one is?"

"Glad to," Katherine called back. "Wow, that's a whopper of a moth," she said when she caught up to them. "I hope it's in the guidebook. They say this book has all the butterflies and moths in the exhibit, but I haven't seen anything like this one." She flipped quickly through the pages. "Moths . . . brown . . . large . . . okay, here we are. That is a—hang on . . ."

As Katherine was talking, the moth landed in the center of Daria's upraised palm. Slowly Daria lowered her hand, and everyone clustered around to see.

"It's kind of weird-looking," said Grace. She sounded disappointed. "Look how fat its body is. Kind of like a cigar."

"Moths have thicker bodies than butterflies do," said Willow, who had just joined the group. "And their bodies have fur, or anyway it looks like fur."

"Do moths always have a mark on their fur that looks like a skull, like this one?" asked Megan. She shuddered. "Creepy!"

"That's not a *skull*," said Lucy. Then she leaned forward to take a closer look at the moth. "Wait. It does kind of look like a skull, actually."

It did. Between the moth's wings—where its shoulders would have been if moths had shoulders—was the clear outline of a human skull. Eyes and all.

"Katherine, have you found this guy in the book yet?" said Willow.

"Yes, I have," said Katherine, not very cheerfully. She held up the page for them all to see.

"It's called a death's-head hawk moth," she told them.

"*Ugh!* What a horrible name!" Daria gave her hand a disgusted shake. To Jane's amazement, the moth let out a piercing squeak as it tumbled off. Then it flapped

slowly into the air, still squeaking.

"Death's-head hawk moths can squeak, as I guess you can see," Katherine said. "They're the only kind of moth we know of that can make any kind of sound! Isn't that interesting?"

"I guess," said Lucy. "But maybe we should go see some different bugs."

"Sure!" said Katherine. She looked down at the information pamphlet she'd picked up earlier. "There's an exhibit called 'Fly, oh My,' about houseflies—"

"No houseflies," Jane, Lucy, Megan, and about ten other girls said at once.

"Fine, fine. What about 'Do Bees Have Knees?'"

"I guess," said Jane.

"Sure," Lucy agreed. "As long as it's actually an exhibit about bees and not, like, how insects' legs work."

"It's definitely a bee exhibit," Katherine answered. "I think the curators were just looking for something to rhyme with 'bees.' And 'Do Bees Have Fleas?' wouldn't have sounded too good."

Megan wasn't sure about the bee idea.

"Bees may not have knees, but they do have *stingers*," she pointed out. "What if one of us is allergic to bee stings? Like, what if I am? I could die!"

Katherine looked as if she was trying not to laugh. "Megan, I'm pretty sure the bees aren't flying around loose. But shall we take a vote? Who'd like to go to the bee exhibit next?"

Almost everyone raised her hand.

"Bees it is," said Katherine.

The bee exhibit had a huge flat observation hive along one wall. It was covered with a sheet of clear plastic so thick and secure-looking that even Megan walked up close to check it out.

"There are twenty thousand worker bees in this hive," Willow told them. "And I think you can see where we got the expression 'as busy as bees' from. The hive has one queen, whose only job is to lay eggs all day. But the worker bees have all kinds of stuff to do, starting with making all these six-sided cells out of beeswax."

"What is beeswax, exactly?" asked Grace. "It's not made from bees, is it?"

"No, no," said Katherine. "Beeswax is made by bees. The worker bees kind of—what's a good way to put this? They kind of sweat the wax out through their stomachs. Then they collect it and use it to build all those cells."

She pointed at one corner of the hive. "That's the nursery. When the queen lays an egg, the workers bring it to a cell over here to hatch. See how there's a tiny egg inside each cell? And then over here is all the honey, of course." Thousands of beeswax cells were dripping with honey in the center of the hive. "The foraging workers go out and collect nectar that they make into honey."

"How do they get out to *find* nectar?" asked Jane.

"Oh, they're not trapped in that hive! It has pipes in the ceiling that lead outside. So the bees can come and go."

"But what if the bees sneak out of the pipes?" asked Megan. She was looking worriedly up at the ceiling. "Because I think some of them might want to."

"No, no," Willow answered. "The museum was very careful when they installed the hive."

Megan tried again. "I know, but if there was a storm or something, some of the pipes that lead outside could get loose."

"The museum was very careful about that, too." Now Willow sounded a little impatient. "I'm sure they planned for storms."

"But Willow, look up there!"

Everyone's eyes followed Megan's pointing finger. And everyone saw that this time, at least, she was right to worry. A line of bees was crawling along the ceiling. As they watched, one of the bees rose into the air and slowly began to fly around the room. Then another, and a third.

"*That's* not part of the exhibit, is it?" said Megan in a wavering voice.

"Hmmm." Willow glanced over at Katherine. The other leader looked toward the exit in a meaningful way.

"I think," said Willow, "that it's time to see another part of the museum. Let's *calmly* and *quietly* go and get our—*No, Megan!* Stay calm, I said!"

But it was too late. Megan was racing for the door.

"I just got stung!" she screeched. "Bee attack! Bee attack!"

Her panic was contagious. The whole pack of girls thundered after her. Behind them, Willow was yelling, "Girls, slow down! Go in single file! *Calmly!*"

It was only a second or two before everyone was out of the bee exhibit and back in the hall, including the leaders. Jane noticed that both Katherine and Willow were panting as if they too had been running hard.

Katherine smoothed her hair and took a deep breath.

"That was stupid of all of us," she said. "The bees weren't chasing us. They were just flying around."

"Well, they're not supposed to be flying around," snapped Daria. "That's the whole point of keeping them behind glass."

Katherine didn't acknowledge her comment.

"And what about my bee sting?" whimpered Megan. "I might be about to have an allergic reaction!"

"Oh, my. Let's take a look at that sting," said Katherine.

Megan stuck her arm out for inspection. "It's right there. Right on my elbow. See the swelling? Oh, I can't stand the sight of it." To prove her point, she shut her eyes.

Katherine looked closely at Megan's elbow. Finally, she said, "It's not swollen. I don't even see a mark."

Megan's eyes popped open. "Yes, you do! Look!" She jammed her elbow closer to Katherine's eyes.

"I really don't see anything there, Megan. Are you sure you got stung?"

"It just looks like a regular elbow. It's not even scraped," Lucy added.

"You imagined it," Daria said coldly.

"I did *not* imagine it! I felt the bee's little legs crawling on me! Then it stung me over and over!"

Megan's face was turning red from embarrassment and anger. She opened her mouth to say more, but Katherine cut her off. "In any case, it's a good thing the exhibit isn't open to the public yet. Willow and I will be sure to let the museum officials know about this tomorrow so they can make repairs."

"And right now I think it's time for some dinner," said Willow. "Why don't we head to the restaurant? If we notice anything interesting along the way, we can always stop to take a look."

"Want to look at 'Insect Predators'?" Willow asked hopefully a minute or so later, pointing at a room guarded by the huge model of a praying mantis.

No one wanted to meet any insect predators.

"What about 'Ladybugs and Other Beetles'?" suggested Katherine when they passed the next gallery. "Or 'Insect-Eating Plants'?"

"Or what about 'Humans Eating Dinner'?" said Lucy's friend Grace. And the rest of the group agreed.

After a few minutes of walking, Jane suddenly

felt something in her shoe. She stopped and leaned up against the wall so she could take the shoe off and shake it. Nothing came out. Jane pressed her foot to the ground and realized that whatever the thing was, it was in her sock.

She sighed with irritation and bent over to pull her sock off. When she turned it inside out, a tiny stone flew out.

That was a relief—but now the group of girls had rounded a corner and disappeared from view. Jane pulled her sock and shoe back on and jogged down the long corridor after them.

At the end of the corridor, she paused. Which way had they gone? She couldn't hear them. Should she yell to see where they were?

I can't start yelling for them, she decided. *It would be too embarrassing.* She would just turn left and see what happened.

It was dumb to be worried, Jane knew. There was no way the group could have gotten so far ahead that she'd lost them. Still, she found herself walking faster and faster. Willow had been right—the place really was like a maze. And Jane had done the one thing Willow had warned against. She'd gone off by herself. Well, not exactly gone off, but . . .

Okay, going left wasn't going to work. She'd have to retrace her steps. Jane turned around.

And from out of nowhere, a monster lunged toward her.

CHAPTER 3

Jane was just opening her mouth to scream when the monster reached up and lifted its face off . . . and there stood Lucy, holding a huge rubber mask and doubling over with laughter.

"You—you—," Jane sputtered. "Where did you *get* that thing?"

"I grabbed it out of the housefly exhibit when we passed it," said Lucy offhandedly. "I think it's supposed to show you what life looks like to a fly. Try it on!"

"No way! Go put it back!"

"I'll put it back *after* you try it on," said Lucy. "Fly eyes are cool. Really, try it!"

Reluctantly Jane pulled the mask over her head.

When she looked through the eyes, she realized what Lucy had meant. It was like looking at the world through dozens of prisms, and all the colors seemed different somehow. But she couldn't appreciate the view when she knew she wasn't supposed to be seeing it.

"All right, fine. Very interesting," Jane said as she yanked off the rubber mask. "Now take it back where it belongs."

Lucy sighed. "Allllllll riiiiiight. If you say so. Wait here for me, okay? Then we can catch up with the others. I know the way to the restaurant."

No one seemed to have noticed that they'd been missing for a few minutes. The rest of the girls were passing a huge replica of a spider when Jane and Lucy caught up.

"Let's stop here for one second," said Willow. "We really shouldn't leave without at least looking at some of the spiders."

There were loud sighs from the girls, but Willow and Katherine were firm. "We'll just look at the first room of the exhibit," said Katherine. "For five minutes only."

The theme of the first room was 'Webs, Nets, and Parachutes—Amazing Spider Silk!' Jane was glad spiders

35

didn't scare her, because some of the webs in the exhibit really *were* amazing. There was even a polyester replica of a very big and very strong spider web—forty feet across. "From the Darwin's bark spider in Madagascar," Katherine told them. "In the wild, some of the webs are eighty feet long. That's as long as two school buses!" Jane was especially interested in the trapdoor spider. Trapdoor spiders, she learned, dug tiny, perfect burrows. They lined them with silk and then used the silk to attach a hinged door to cover the burrow's hole. They also raised their globe-shaped spiderlings in the tunnel, feeding them left-over insects.

"The babies are actually kind of cute," Jane marveled as she stared into the glass case holding an actual trap-door spider.

"So small, too," said Lucy. "They're the size of a cake sprinkle!"

Daria was peering over Lucy's shoulder to see. "I just heard someone say that you're never farther than seven feet away from a spider," she reported. "No matter where you are—inside, outside, underground . . ."

"That can't be right," said Lucy. "Look around this room! Well, I mean, not this room, because after all, this *is* a spider exhibit. But if we go into—say—the middle of the Great Hall—or my family room—there won't be a spider seven feet away."

"How do you know? Look how tiny these baby spiders are. Maybe you just don't see them."

For some reason, Jane's skin suddenly began to itch. She didn't hate spiders, but she didn't like them, either, and the idea that one might be close enough to crawl on her really creeped her out. To her relief, Willow called out to the group.

"I know we said we just wanted to show you one room . . ."

More groans from the girls.

"But they did give me and Katherine permission to take out one of the tarantulas. Does anyone want to see it? It's in a tank in the next room. Anyone who's interested, come with me. The rest of you can wait in here with Katherine."

About twenty girls followed Willow, including Megan.

"I wouldn't have thought you were interested in tarantulas, Megan," Lucy said.

"I'm *not*! But it would be way *worse* to stay in the other room waiting and waiting and wondering what would happen if the tarantula broke free and viciously attacked everyone."

"Tarantulas are actually harmless," said Willow, who had overheard this. "Nothing to worry about. They're even kind of cuddly, if you look closely." She had reached a row of glass tanks and was lifting the wire top off one of them. "Hey, buddy," she said. "Ready to make some friends?" Gently she lifted out the creature inside.

Even Jane caught her breath when she saw the tarantula. Its furry black body was the size of two plums, and its legs were about six inches long.

"This is Trudy." Willow lightly stroked the tarantula's back. "Her species is found in South America, and she eats mostly cockroaches. Does anyone have any questions about her?"

"How does she spray her deadly poison?" asked one girl named Stella.

Willow laughed. "Tarantulas aren't poisonous! Except to their prey. They do sometimes bite, but their bite is no more dangerous than a bee sting."

Megan had lurked in the doorway instead of fully

coming into the room. Now she took a giant step backward.

"But they only bite the insects they catch," Willow continued. "Or—in the case of really big tarantulas—the mice and birds."

Megan took another step backward.

"*That's* not a big tarantula?" asked Lucy. "She looks huge to me."

"Some tarantulas are as big as dinner plates," Willow told her. "They're big enough to eat snakes."

Megan stepped back yet again—and tripped.

"*Watch out!*" called Willow. "The spider web is right behind you!"

Megan had stumbled only inches from the forty-foot fake web in the first room. She threw out a hand to break her fall—and her arm went right through the web. She grabbed the web with her other hand—and the whole web collapsed on her.

Willow leaped forward to help. The sudden movement must have startled the tarantula, who fell off Willow's hand and began to scuttle away.

"EVERYBODY FREEZE!" Willow yelled at the top of her lungs. "Or you'll step on Trudy!"

Of course all the girls had been about to scatter—but now they halted instantly. Only Trudy continued her skittering path across the floor.

"She's coming for me! She's going to attack!" Megan wailed. She tried to jump to her feet but only managed to get herself more tangled in the giant web.

"She is *not* going to attack," said Willow. "She's much more scared than you are. Hold still, everyone—and you, too, Megan. I need to pick her up."

She walked calmly over to the tarantula and scooped her up. Just as calmly, she brought her back to the tank and closed the lid. Jane was sure she was just imagining things, but it seemed like the tarantula was happy to be back in its cage. Then at last she turned toward Megan.

Katherine had reached Megan by then and was kneeling on the floor beside her. "Megan, could you try to stop squirming around?" she said. "You're just getting more tangled."

"I bet *you'd* squirm if millions of poisonous spiders were attacking you!" said Megan tearfully.

Katherine looked over at Willow and sighed. "This will be hard to explain to the staff," she said.

"I think it's good that it happened," said Lucy. "If

that web could fall on Megan, it could fall on anyone. The museum people should be *glad* it happened before the exhibit was open to the public. Someone could have gotten hurt!"

"How do you know I didn't get hurt?" complained Megan.

"Well, did you?"

"No, I guess not." Megan sounded disappointed. "I could have, though."

Willow's voice was brisk. "But you didn't. And neither did Trudy. And if we all work at it, we can get you untangled before you know it."

"Wow, this is amazing," Jane said fifteen minutes later.

"I think it's *horrible*," said Megan. "What if it springs a leak?"

The group had untangled Megan, folded up the fake web, and then gone on to dinner, hungrier than ever. Now they were in the Templeton Museum's restaurant, which had been built to look like a submarine. The walls were lined with portholes that showed superrealistic fish "swimming" past the sub. As the girls watched, a cloud of transparent jellyfish floated from one porthole to the next. The jellyfish were followed by a huge hammerhead shark. After the shark, a squid shot past. Starfish crept up the portholes and vanished from view. A school of seahorses wriggled by. Jane was pretty sure that none of these sea creatures shared the same spots in the same ocean, but who cared? As long as a mermaid didn't show up, it was easy to believe they were really underwater.

In the front of the sub, Katherine and Willow were setting out pans of lasagna, stacks of garlic bread, and a huge bowl of salad. "Come and get it, girls!" called Katherine. "After you've served yourselves, you can sit wherever you want."

Jane and Lucy ended up sitting with a bunch of Lucy's friends, plus Megan. At the last minute, Daria also plunked herself down at their table. From her expression, she seemed to think she was doing them a favor.

Lucy, Grace, and Cailyn all went to the same school. They knew Megan and the other girls at the table from summer programs at the museum.

"Where do you live, Jane?" asked Cailyn.

Jane could feel herself blushing. "I . . . I know this

sounds stupid, but I don't remember the address. We just got here."

"Well, do you know where you'll be going to school?" Cailyn pressed.

"I don't think I'll be going to school," Jane confessed. She hated the way everyone was staring at her. "My mother . . ." She trailed off.

"Oh, you're homeschooled!" said Cailyn, and Jane nodded uncertainly.

"Lots of kids around here are homeschooled," Grace told her. "That's why a lot of them come to the classes and stuff here at the museum—it's a good way to meet kids their own age."

"That must be the *only* thing this museum is good for," said Daria.

"Give it a chance!" protested Lucy. "We haven't seen any of the real stuff yet. Like the new Egyptian wing."

"Big deal. Lots of museums have Egyptian exhibits," said Daria with a sniff.

"Yeah, but this one's been totally fixed up and added to. Willow said the museum bought the whole collection of an Egyptian museum that had to close for some reason. They got tons of stuff from some royal tombs that were discovered about twenty years ago. And solid-gold jewelry and papyrus scrolls and . . . oh, you know, royal pottery and things. And a *lot* of mummies. Now only two other museums in the country have bigger Egyptian exhibits than Templeton."

"I love Egyptian stuff," said Grace. "We did a whole unit on ancient Egypt last year. We each got assigned a character that we had to study and then pretend to be. I was a pharaoh." She giggled. "People had to obey my every command."

"There weren't any girl pharaohs," said Daria.

"Yes, there were! Not a lot of them, but a couple," Grace answered. "We studied that exact thing." She stopped to take a bite of lasagna. "Mmm, this is really good."

Daria didn't seem to agree about the museum's food, either. She wasn't eating much, Jane noticed—just pushing things around on her plate with a discontented face. Jane wondered why Daria was even *at* the lock-in if she hated everything so much. Maybe her mother had made her come, the way Jane's had. But even if she didn't want to be here, couldn't she try to be nice?

For the first time since she'd signed in, Jane suddenly

got up the nerve to start a conversation. A conversation about the one thing that had been secretly haunting her all day.

"*I've* heard something interesting about the Templeton Museum," she blurted out. "That it's haunted."

Everyone at the table stopped eating and stared at her.

"That's what they say," said Jane more quietly. "In fact, it's the Egyptian exhibit that's supposed to be haunted. People say that one of the mummies comes to life every night."

"Don't be ridiculous," said Daria.

"It's true! I mean, it's true that it's what I've heard," Jane said more carefully. "I mean it could be just a story, but—"

"Of course it's just a story," said Daria.

"Well, then, the *story* is that this mummy comes to life every night and walks through the museum."

Megan looked as if she was about to cry.

But Grace looked excited. "Ooooh," she said. "I like that kind of story."

All the girls at the table were leaning their heads in closer to listen.

"Who told you such a stupid lie?" asked Daria.

"Actually, it was—" Jane stopped midsentence. Her mother had told her the story. But it would sound so babyish to say that out loud.

"I've just heard people talking about it," Jane said weakly.

"Why would a mummy do something as *stupid* as walking around this *stupid* place?" asked Daria.

"Why not?" Grace snapped. "It would be a lot more interesting than lying on the floor in a casket or whatever."

Daria pushed her chair back to stand up. "You're all crazy. I'm moving to another table."

Lucy's cheeks had turned red, and her eyes were bright with fury. She'd finally had enough of Daria's attitude. "You're just scared!" she accused.

Daria plunked herself back down into her seat. "I'm what?"

"It's all right, Lucy," said Jane quietly. "Just forget about it."

But Lucy was obviously too mad to stop. "I said, 'You're just scared!' Too scared even to listen. I bet Jane is right. This museum has a lot of weird history. Why *shouldn't* a mummy be haunting it?"

"Because Jane is just making it up, that's why." Daria's smooth, fake-grown-up voice was infuriating.

"I'm not making it up!" Jane said. "I swear I'm not!"

"Then prove it!" Daria shot back.

"I . . . I . . ." Jane faltered. "There's no way I can prove something like that. How could anyone—"

"Oh, giiiiiirls!" Katherine's voice suddenly trilled through the air. She was standing up by the buffet tables. "Dessert's ready! Or should I say, *lots* of desserts are ready? Come help yourselves! There are make-your-own sundaes and brownies and cupcakes and lemon squares and—"

The rest of her sentence was cut off as people jumped up and rushed toward the desserts. Megan, finally happy, was the first one in line.

But Daria didn't move from her place. Her eyes were still fixed on Jane and Lucy.

"You can prove it by coming on a midnight hunt for the mummy," she said in a low voice. "We'll go after everyone's asleep."

"But why should I?" asked Jane. "I didn't say I believed that there's a mummy, only that I heard a rumor."

47

Daria didn't argue with her. She didn't say anything at all, or even blink, until finally she slowly mouthed the word *chicken* at Jane.

How did I get myself into this? Jane thought, anguished.

She had just wanted to shut Daria up. Instead she had . . . *wound* her up!

"I dare you, chicken," taunted Daria.

"You know what, *I'll* take you up on that dare," Lucy suddenly said. "Only Jane, you really should come along too," she added in her regular, not-mad voice. "It'll be fun."

Fun? Fun walking around in a deserted museum after dark? Fun breaking the rules? Fun looking for a *mummy*?

But after all, Jane reminded herself, *I was the one who started this.* And she didn't want to seem scared of her own shadow, like Megan.

"Of course I'll come," she heard herself saying.

"Do you both promise?" asked Daria.

"We promise," Jane and Lucy answered together.

"Good. I'll put my blankets near yours. As soon as everyone is sleeping, we'll set out." Daria's voice was firm. Very firm.

"Come on, slowpokes," called Willow. "The ice cream is melting!"

But Jane had totally lost her appetite. As she trailed along behind the others, she stared unseeingly at the fake portholes on the walls. She hoped against hope that Daria just fell asleep later and didn't make them follow through on the dare. After all, she didn't know which was worse: actually seeing a mummy, or Daria making fun of her mercilessly for bringing it up.

CHAPTER 4

"And this is some of the treasure the explorers found," explained Willow.

After dinner, the group had continued its tour of the museum. After going through the Hall of Mythology, they soon wandered into the Egyptian wing—an exhibit that the group leaders said would be fun to walk through before heading back to the Great Hall for bed. And it *was* fun, even though Jane wasn't exactly in the mood to think about ancient Egypt. Right now the girls were looking at a room filled with treasure. Daria didn't seem impressed, but Jane was sure she was faking it. How could anybody not be impressed? The room wasn't that big, but it was filled with actual heaps of gold—like a hoard in a fairy tale. There were hammered bracelets, necklaces of gold and turquoise beads, gold chains, jeweled hair ornaments, gold sandals, even what must have been a solid-gold chair.

"There's lots more gold. But this is what the archaeologists found in the outer chamber when they unsealed the tomb in 1932," said Katherine.

"Broke into the tomb and robbed it, you mean," Jane heard Daria mutter.

There was no way Katherine could have heard Daria, who was all the way in the back with Jane, but as if by coincidence, Katherine went on to explain, "Today's archaeologists do believe that tomb robbers tried to steal this treasure—but centuries ago, not in 1932. Treasure wouldn't have been piled up this way by the ancient Egyptians. It would have been arranged neatly near the caskets of the people who were expected to use it in the next life. It *definitely* wouldn't have been left by the outer door. The thieves may have been startled by a noise. They dumped the gold, resealed the tomb, and ran off. And no one found the tomb again for almost three thousand years."

Now Willow took up the story. "The tomb had been

carved out of a cliff. It had about thirty rooms, so we know it must have belonged to an important king. Let's go into the next gallery and find out more."

"Sar-co-pha-gus," Willow pronounced in a teacherish way a few seconds later. She gestured down at the vast alabaster form lying on the floor in front of them. A row of similar objects had been arranged down one wall of the room. "A sarcophagus is a stone case that holds a coffin, inside a coffin, that's sometimes inside *another* coffin. This sarcophagus belonged to Prince Amun, one of the pharaoh's seven sons."

"Is the prince *in* there?" Megan asked her.

Willow chuckled. "Well, his mummy is. That's the whole point of a sarcophagus!"

Megan took a couple of steps backward.

"Why weren't ordinary coffins enough to hold the bodies?" asked Jane. "It's not as if the people inside them were going anywhere. The regular coffins didn't need to be put into *stone* coffins."

"Ancient Egyptians believed bodies needed extra protection after death," said Katherine. "Since they were going on a trip to the afterlife, they needed to be in good shape when they arrived."

Jane couldn't help but wonder if one of the mummies in this room was getting ready to pop out of its sarcophagus.

She hoped against hope that all the layers of coffins would keep the mummy from getting up and walking around the museum that night.

"Do you think Prince What's-his-name is in good, uh, shape in there?" asked Jane.

Willow paused before answering. "I guess that depends on what you call 'good shape,'" she finally said. "Ancient Egypt was hot and dry. That would preserve a body pretty well on its own. And the meticulous mummification process definitely helped too. But I'm guessing that his body is probably . . . um, not quite . . . Let me put it this way. He's not going to get up and walk out of this room."

Jane saw Lucy cringe ever so slightly at Willow's comment. She couldn't help glancing at Daria. But the other girl was staring down at Prince Amun's sarcophagus. Jane couldn't see her expression.

"Who's in these other sarcophaguses?" asked Grace.

"Sarcophagi," Willow corrected her. "They all belong to different members of Egyptian royal families. Prince

Amun's wife is next to him, and the Prince's brother and *his* wife are next to them. Then there are a bunch of more distant relatives."

Lucy, who had wandered a little way off, hadn't been paying attention to the last part. "What are these *little* sarcophaguses for? And why do they have animal heads?" She pointed at a glass case holding a row of heavy stone jars about a foot high.

"Sarcophagi," Willow said again. "But they're not sarcophagi. They're canopic jars."

"What are—"

"Why don't you just read the card?" Daria interrupted.

Lucy made a little face. But she turned to the placard on the wall and began to read aloud. "'Canopic jars were used during mummification. They held the organs of . . . Oh, gross! These jars have *guts* in them!"

"They're probably empty now," said Katherine. "But yes, each mummy needed four canopic jars to store the body's organs. Ancient Egyptians believed that people's bodies would need them when they arrived in the afterlife. The stomach, intestines, liver, and lungs each went into a different jar. The heart stayed in the body, though."

"That makes me feel *so* much better," said Cailyn sarcastically.

"And what are these eagle mummies doing here?" Lucy pointed at two small coffins hanging on the wall.

"Egyptians mummified all kinds of animals," said Willow. "Both wild animals and pets. Even donkeys, sometimes, in case a person might need a ride in the afterlife."

"Ancient Egyptians thought way too much about being dead," said Jane.

"Okay, girls. Listen up," Willow said, once they were settled back into the Great Hall. "We don't expect you to fall asleep right away. But try not to stay up too late, okay? We're going to keep the lights on for an hour." She pointed to a huge clock on the wall above the east entrance. "And then, after we turn off the lights, you can *whisper* for another hour. But after that, we want you to go to sleep."

Which was not what happened.

"And when they found her, she was missing her *head!*" Grace whispered two hours later.

Katherine and Willow, at least, had fallen asleep. The two of them lay hunched and quiet in their sleeping bags in the center of the Great Hall. But they were the only ones in the room who were sleeping.

The lights had been turned off more than an hour before. But the little lights marking the doorways were glowing dimly. They made the Great Hall look shadowy and strange—a good background for the scary stories Lucy and a cluster of other girls were telling. Jane hadn't contributed any, but she'd been listening, riveted, as the stories got wilder and wilder. Daria hadn't contributed either, but Jane had the feeling that she wasn't missing a word.

"I bet that's not true about the girl's head," Cailyn said now. "A person's head can't fall off from terror."

"It can too!" Grace said indignantly. "It happened to my cousin's friend's best *friend*!"

Cailyn yawned. "Yeah, right. People always say something happened to a friend of a friend of a third cousin or something. I'll believe it when you say it happened to *you*."

"But then how could I say it? I wouldn't have a head," Grace retorted. The other girls started to laugh.

"All right, it's Cailyn's turn to tell a story," Lucy said once the giggles had died down. "Tell us something scary that happened to you!"

"Okay. But I need licorice first." Jane passed her the pack, and Cailyn pried a strand loose. "Well, *muh* muh wuh—"

"Gross! Finish chewing first!" Lucy ordered.

"'Kay." Cailyn swallowed and started over. "First of all, this was something that happened when I was six, before I knew any of you. At our old house. My parents were out late at a party, and they had hired a babysitter named Traci.

"I don't know where my parents found Traci," Cailyn continued, "but she was a totally horrible babysitter. I mean *totally*. She told me it was time for bed when it was only six thirty. When I said that I knew how to tell time and that I didn't have to go to bed for another hour and a half, Traci said, 'Well, *I'm* tired. I'm going to take a nap on the sofa. Just don't do anything bad while I'm sleeping.'"

"And you didn't, because you're such a goody-goody," Grace added.

"No, I really didn't. I behaved myself the whole time

she was snoring away. But I did check the refrigerator to see what kind of snacks my parents had left for Traci. They always gave babysitters way better snacks than they gave *us*."

The other girls nodded in sympathy.

"So there was this huge slab of chocolate cake from the bakery," said Cailyn. "I figured it was *so* big that Traci wouldn't notice if I tried a little slice. I went and got a plate and a fork. And while I was cutting off a little piece of cake, I heard something behind me.

"I guess my conscience was bothering me, because I thought it must be Traci. I whipped around, but no one was behind me. But at the window . . ." Cailyn stopped to take another bite of red licorice.

"What? *What* was at the window?" asked several voices.

"Nothing. I didn't see anything."

"Wow, this is so terrifying," said Grace sarcastically, rolling her eyes.

"At least it's realistic," Lucy added.

"Just wait," said Cailyn. "I'm getting to the scary part. So I got my cake and went to the table to eat it. Our kitchen table was in this kind of—kind of nook thing with three windows, one on each side. And while I was eating, I heard the sound again. A scratching sound. From the window behind me. So naturally I whipped around again—and I saw a stick scraping against the window."

Grace groaned. "A tree. Woo-hooo!"

"No," said Cailyn. *"There was someone holding the stick."*

Now she had their attention.

"I could see the person's arm—a black sleeve and a hand in a black glove. A *huge* glove, like the person was really, really big. But it was too dark for me to see the rest of him. He scraped the stick across the window again. And then he tapped with it—three times. *Tap-tap-tap.* And then I saw them . . . eyes. Bright white eyes with light blue pupils . . . so light they looked almost white too.

"But his eyes were all I saw. He must have been wearing some kind of black hood thing over his face—you know, that kind of hat-mask thing that goes over your head and has holes for the eyes and mouth?"

"A balaclava," said one girl in a know-it-all voice. Everyone shushed her. Jane realized that they were now the center of a big group. A lot more girls had pulled up their sleeping bags to listen to Cailyn's story.

"His eyes were so weird," Cailyn whispered. "I know I was only six, but I still remember them. They were *so white*. And they were staring right at me.

"I opened my mouth to call Traci, but it was like one of those nightmares—you know, the ones where you try to talk but you can't? I could only make this little croaking sound.

"He lifted up his other hand, and I saw that he was holding a hammer. He held it up as if he was going to smash the window—but then all he did was tap the glass with it. *Tap-tap-tap. Tap-tap-tap.*"

"And while I was looking at the hammer, his other hand suddenly smashed through the glass. AND HE KILLED ME!"

As she shrieked the last words, Cailyn lunged at Grace's throat.

Jane screamed. So did everyone else who'd been listening to the story. Which made the rest of the girls in the Great Hall scream, even Daria. Which woke up Willow and Katherine—who also screamed.

Abruptly the overhead lights came on. And a man's voice yelled, "What's going on? What's the matter?"

Standing in the west doorway were two museum

guards. Both were panting from having run so fast.

"Uh-oh," Lucy muttered. "Busted."

Now the chaperones were both standing up. Even though the lights were on, Katherine was aiming her flashlight all around like a TV cop. "What happened, girls?" she asked.

I'll get us out of this, Jane thought. She was very proud of how not-shy she was growing as the night's festivities went on.

She raised her hand. "It's—it's all my fault," she said apologetically. "I get nightmares. I must have screamed in my sleep."

Lucy chimed in loyally. "And then I heard her, and it made *me* scream. And then I guess everyone got scared."

"*You* got scared," said one of the guards. "I almost had a heart attack when we heard you. Try and keep it down for the rest of the night, okay?"

"We're so sorry, officers," said Katherine, who still seemed to think she was in a TV show. "We won't let it happen again."

"Thanks," the other guard said curtly.

"Well, girls," Willow said sternly when the guards

were gone. "That was an embarrassment. You're too old for this kind of thing. I want everyone to settle down *now*."

"People can't help having nightmares," Katherine pointed out. She looked kindly at Jane. "Would you like to move your sleeping bag over next to us, Jane? That might make things seem less scary."

"Um—no, that's okay," said Jane. "I'm fine. Really."

"Please *stay* fine," said Willow. "I'm turning the lights off now, and I don't want to hear another sound until morning."

She snapped off the lights.

For a few seconds there was total silence. Then Lucy whispered, "Good job, Cailyn."

"You have to admit it scared you," Cailyn hissed back.

"QUIET," Willow blared. "*Go. To. Sleep.*"

And now, at last, the Great Hall actually quieted down. There were a few more whispered giggles. A few rearrangements of sleeping bags and thumpings of pillows. Then, gradually, the room filled with the soft, even breathing sound of people falling asleep.

Jane was relieved. Now maybe Lucy and Daria would

just forget about settling their bet. Jane felt so comfortable just lying here. She could feel her eyelids getting heavy. . . .

And then Lucy nudged her in the side. "Jane!" she whispered. "Are you awake?"

"No," said Jane sleepily.

"Well, *be* awake! We have to look for the mummy, remember? Daria's ready to go."

Jane groaned. "Can't you and Daria just go together without me?"

"No way!" whispered Lucy. "We need you as a witness! Besides, it won't be fun for me unless you come."

"All right." Jane rolled over and sat up. On Lucy's other side, Daria was already sitting up.

"Wait!" whispered Lucy. "I need to get my flashlight."

"What *is* this obsession with all the flashlights?" said Daria impatiently. "There are *real* lights all over the museum!"

"I'm not wandering around this building without a flashlight," Lucy said. She burrowed through her backpack until she found it. "Okay, let's go."

Slowly, the three girls stood up. *Good so far,* Jane thought. No one around them had moved. She pointed at the nearest exit. *That one?* she mouthed.

Lucy shook her head. *THAT one,* she mouthed back, jerking her head toward the north doorway.

Jane's heart sank. The door Lucy wanted was all the way across the Great Hall! They would have to make their way around so many people, and they would have to pass the leaders. But she could hardly start arguing now. She took a deep breath and began tiptoeing behind Lucy and Daria.

All around them, girls lay sound asleep. Grace was lying on her back, halfway out of her sleeping bag. Cailyn was rolled into a ball with one hand sticking out. She was still holding that licorice, Jane noticed.

Oh, if only Lucy and Daria hadn't gotten into that argument! If only she had never mentioned the stupid mummy. Everyone looked so cozy here. *I hope we see the mummy fast and get it over with,* thought Jane. But wait—that wasn't the thing to wish for. She didn't *want* to see a mummy.

On the other hand, at least if they did see a mummy, they'd be able to go back to bed.

On the other hand, what if they saw a mummy and it attacked them?

On the other hand, if a real mummy was actually roaming around, wasn't it better to be awake? What would prevent the mummy from coming into the Great Hall and doing whatever it was mummies did to their victims? Did mummies *have* victims? What exactly did mummies do besides shuffle around and groan?

While she'd been worrying about all this, Jane hadn't noticed how far she and the other two girls were advancing. They were almost at the north doorway now. Another thirty feet or so, and they'd be safe. Maybe this wouldn't be so—

At that moment Lucy gasped. Jane turned to see what she was looking at—and stopped in her tracks.

Willow was sitting up. And she was staring straight at them!

CHAPTER 5

The three girls froze in midstep. Jane's heart was pounding so hard she could barely breathe.

As they watched, breathless, Willow raised one hand and pointed at them.

"*You.*"

Then—

"You left it at the store," Willow said in a blurry voice thick with sleep. And she lay down again.

Lucy let out a long breath. "She must be dreaming," she whispered. "Let's get out of here."

Jane glanced around, but no one seemed to have woken up. Silently the girls tiptoed out of the Great Hall. In the corridor they broke into a run. When they were safely out of range, Lucy doubled over with quiet laughter.

"'You left it at the store,'" she said. "Don't you wish we could ask her what 'it' was?"

But Jane felt too rattled to laugh. "We could have gotten out of the Great Hall in two seconds if we'd used the closest door. Why did you make us walk all the way across the room like that?" she asked.

"To give us more of an adventure!" said Lucy. "And you have to admit, it was more exciting my way. Now come on, let's get started on our hunt."

"Get started how?" said Jane. "What are we supposed to do—just wander around the museum hoping to see a mummy?"

"We'll go back to the Egyptian exhibit, of course," said Lucy. "Where else would a mummy hang around?"

"No." Daria's voice was firm. "If there is a mummy, do you think it would really hang out in the Egyptian exhibit every night? It would want to explore. It could be anywhere. We should start on the third floor and work our way down. It's more organized that way."

"The *third floor*? But then we'll be really far away from the Great Hall. We'll never be able to outrun the guards if they suspect us!" said Jane in a panicky voice.

Daria glared at her. "Then go back if you're so scared."

"No, no, no, I'm fine," Jane said hastily. Going back alone would be even worse than going up to the third floor. "Sounds great. Let's go!"

She strode purposefully toward the stairs.

At the top of the second flight the girls stopped to check the information map on the wall. It was hard to know where to start. "What about the medieval jewelry?" asked Jane hopefully.

"Actually, can we check out the Arms and Armor exhibit first?" said Lucy. "That's my favorite. I was bummed we didn't go there earlier tonight. Then I think we should look in the dinosaur wing. Dinosaurs and mummies have a lot in common—you know, being all bones and everything."

The Arms and Armor hall held an entire battalion. A long row of knights in armor, seated on horses in armor, had been set up to look as if they were marching down the center of the vast floor. The knights were posed for battle, or for a parade. Their horses were made of some kind of cloth that had been molded over a frame, but they were amazingly realistic all the same. Each knight held a long wooden pike in its right hand. Each horse stood in exactly the same pose.

The endless procession gave Jane a strange, lonely feeling. Those poor knights! They would be marching, marching, marching until the end of time without ever arriving.

Even Daria seemed interested. She moved up close to one knight to examine his armor in the dim light. "Their *gloves* were made of metal," she said, peering at the knight closest to her. "How could they move their fingers?"

"It says here that armor was easier to move in than people think." Lucy was reading a plaque on the wall. "It wasn't as heavy as people think, either. A full suit of armor weighed less than what a firefighter wears now. What I wonder about are the horses. I just feel so bad for them having had to wear all that metal."

"I wish they weren't so tall," Lucy added regretfully. "Every time I come in here, I want to lift up one of those visors and peek inside. Maybe there would be an old knight's skull grinning out at us. Hey! A mummy couldn't climb inside a suit of armor, could it?"

"I'll look inside," said Daria. And before either Jane or Lucy realized what she was doing or could stop her,

Daria had vaulted up onto the back of one of the armored horses and sat down behind the suit of armor.

She grinned smugly down at them from her perch.

"Get down from there! *Get down!*" said Lucy frantically. "You'll set off the alarm!"

But amazingly, no alarm rang. Maybe it hadn't occurred to the museum that anyone might actually climb onto one of the horses.

"You can't be up there!" hissed Jane.

"Too bad. I *am* up here." Daria reached around and opened the knight's visor. Since she was sitting behind him, of course she couldn't see inside his helmet.

"Lucy, look inside and tell me what you see in there," Daria ordered.

"How?" Lucy asked. "I'm nowhere near tall enough to see in there."

Besides, thought Jane, *what if she peeks inside and a mummy pops out? That would just about scare me to death.*

But Daria wouldn't accept any excuses. "Jane can hold you up."

"What? No, I can't," said Jane.

"I'm not coming down until you look inside this knight's helmet," said Daria. "I dare you."

"Not again. This is ridiculous," said Jane in despair. "Lucy, let's just get out of here."

"No, no," said Lucy. "Just hold me up for one second. I'll look inside the visor."

Jane sighed. The night wasn't going to go very well if Daria kept daring Lucy to do things. "Well, I'm not lifting you," she told Lucy. "I'll get on my hands and knees and you can stand on my back."

"Ouch," she said a second later, as first one and then the other of Lucy's feet pressed heavily down on her back.

Above her, she heard a metallic creak as Lucy lifted the knight's visor again. Then a metallic clang as she dropped it shut. Then the welcome thud as Lucy jumped back onto the floor.

And then the very *unwelcome* sound of the sword from the knight's hand clattering to the floor.

Jane straightened up hastily just as Daria hopped off the horse's back. The three girls looked uneasily at one another, and then at the entrance.

When no guard came rushing in, the girls turned back to the sword.

"It must have been loose," said Jane. She didn't sound very sure.

"Not glued in very well, I guess," said Lucy.

"So what do you want to do about it?" asked Daria. "Should we try to put it back?"

Jane glared at Daria. "Thanks for getting us into this mess."

"Lucy's the one who jumped off like a ton of bricks and dislodged the sword," said Daria.

"I'm not putting that sword back," Lucy said. "What if it falls again and hurts someone?"

"Well, we can't just leave it there! They might suspect that someone wandered around alone during the lock-in," Jane pointed out.

Daria's lips tightened. She strode over to the sword and picked it up by the hilt with her finger and thumb. Holding it far away from her, she reached overhead and put it on top of a nearby cabinet.

"There. You can stop worrying," she said. "Tomorrow, write a note saying where it is, then leave the note somewhere that someone's sure to find it."

"Hey, that's not a bad idea," said Lucy approvingly. "We can leave the note at the information desk on our way home. Good! That solves that. And now, back to the mummy. There was nothing inside that armor except stale museum air. Of course, we'd have to check *all* the suits of armor to be sure there's not a mummy inside one of them."

Jane stretched out her aching back. "There isn't a mummy in *any* of them," she snapped. "It would have fallen apart. Mummies are all crumbling and rotting inside those old bandages or whatever they're wrapped in."

"Wrong again," said Daria, whose brief moment of helpfulness seemed to be over. "Egyptian mummies were well preserved. When scientists unwrapped King Ramses, he looked just the way he had when he was alive."

Lucy shook her head. "Except that he was all shriveled up and leathery-looking. And his head looked just like a turtle's head. I've seen pictures in my social studies book."

"What does it matter, anyway?" asked Jane. She didn't want to think about what King Ramses had looked like when he was unwrapped. "Let's move on to the dinosaur exhibit. And *no more dares!*"

"The experts can say whatever they want," said Lucy. "But I say *Tyrannosaurus rex* couldn't have been all that scary in real life. Not with those puny little arms."

"But look at those teeth," Jane pointed out.

The three girls were standing under the hulking form of a T. rex skeleton. Its eyeless skull was glaring down at them. Its teeth—six inches long, the wall placard said—were definitely sharp. But its arms did look kind of useless.

Jane noticed that for the first time all evening, Daria looked impressed. She walked up to get a closer look at the humongous skeleton and read the information on the wall. "It says here that T. rexes had really bad breath," she said. "Their teeth were covered with so much bacteria that they could give their prey a fatal infection. I guess if they didn't eat their prey first."

"*That* I can believe," said Lucy.

The T. rex skeleton had all kinds of company in the room. Compared to some of the other skeletons, it wasn't even that big. One dinosaur's skull brushed the ceiling, and its body was as long as the whole room.

"That isn't a real skeleton," said Daria. "No animal was ever that big."

"That's not what it says here," Lucy replied. She was studying the information card. "This isn't even the biggest dinosaur! They've found one in Argentina that's a hundred and fifty feet long. Just its *spine* weighs a ton. Two thousand pounds!."

Daria looked as if she couldn't even comprehend what Lucy was saying..

"And look at these dino eggs!" said Lucy, stopping by a sheet of petrified mud. Eons earlier, a dinosaur had scratched a little hollow into the mud to use as a nest. "They're almost as big as I am. And this footprint is *bigger* than I am!"

She lay down next to the footprint to prove it, then hopped back to her feet. "Don't they have anything interactive in the dino exhibit? We might as well do something while we're looking around. Let's see what's in the other room."

The next room had tons of interactive stuff, but it was obviously meant for children who were a lot younger than the three girls. For one thing, its main feature was a huge wooden jungle gym shaped like a dinosaur skeleton. There were also tables with dinosaur coloring books and a sandbox where kids could play with plastic toy dinosaurs. Jane noticed that someone had buried a lot of the dinosaurs upside down. There were a bunch of interactive displays, but they were disappointingly babyish. All except one—the replica of a dinosaur skull with very, very pointy teeth.

Can You Imagine? said the plaque next to the skull. *Allosaurus needed these big teeth to chew his food. Dino meat was a lot tougher than a hamburger! You can feel how sharp they are, but be careful!*

Lucy pressed a careful finger onto one of the skull's front teeth. "Yup. Sharp."

"I'll pass," said Jane.

Then Daria reached into the open jaws to touch one of the replica's back teeth—and the jaws snapped shut on her arm.

"Hey!" said Daria. "Is that supposed to happen?" She shook her wrist to free it, but the jaws stayed firmly closed. "What a strange thing to have in a children's room," she said after a second.

"It must be broken. Maybe there's a spring inside or something. Does it hurt?" asked Lucy.

"As a matter of fact, it does," said Daria grimly. With her left hand, she was trying to bend back the top jaw, but it wouldn't budge. "Hey, you two—how about not just *watching* me?"

Jane and Lucy both sprang to help her. "Jane, you

hold that side and I'll hold this one," ordered Lucy. Carefully they grabbed the jaws, trying to keep their fingers clear of those huge teeth. "Daria, you press down on the lower jaw and—"

"And get bitten?" asked Daria angrily. "The only place to press down is onto the teeth!"

"Oh yeah. Sorry," Lucy said. "All right, then, try not to move. Jane, lift your side when I say three. One, two, three!"

They pulled as hard as they could.

"I think it moved a little on my side," Jane said after a few seconds.

"Mine too. I'll count again. One, two . . ."

This time, with a creaking sound, the jaws opened a tiny bit.

"Progress," said Lucy. "Try again."

"And try *faster*. My hand is starting to burn from the pain," said Daria.

On their third try, the jaws finally opened—and Daria slipped her arm out. Both Lucy and Jane gasped when they saw how mangled and red the skin on her arm was.

"We've got to get something to put on that," Lucy

said. "Or at least wash it so that—"

Daria interrupted her. "*Shhhh!* I hear something!"

"Matty? Is that you?"

It was a woman's voice. A guard calling to another guard? It had to be.

"Matty!" the woman said again. "Are you okay?"

Now they could hear footsteps. And they were coming closer.

For the third time the guard called out. Her voice was sharper this time.

"Who's in there? Stay where you are!"

CHAPTER 6

"This way," hissed Daria. She grabbed the hands of the other girls and all but dragged them across the floor.

Through the dim light, Jane realized that they were heading to the dinosaur-shaped play equipment. But they couldn't hide under that. The guard would be able to see right through the ribs!

No, Daria was leading them out through the dinosaur's ribs and to the other side. She pointed with her chin toward what looked like a pile of rocks. After a second, Jane could see that they had an opening that looked like a cave entrance. That must be where Daria wanted them to hide.

Jane's leg slammed hard against something. "Ouch,"

she said in a loud, normal voice.

"Quiet! Get down!" Daria's whisper had the intensity of a shriek. She dropped to her knees and began crawling rapidly toward the play cave. Jane and Lucy followed her.

We can't fit through that, Jane thought in terror. But Daria was scrambling through the entrance with Lucy just behind her. Jane took a breath and crawled in after them. Then, panting, the three of them leaned against the wall of the tiny chamber they had just entered.

It was completely dark. Jane put out a careful hand and touched the wall of the cave. It wasn't rock—it was something that felt fake. She realized that they must be inside some kind of make-believe cave.

"That was lucky," said Lucy. "How did you know this was here?"

Daria shrugged. "I just noticed it. I was—"

Then she stopped.

Someone was walking toward them.

The guard! Jane mouthed silently.

The footsteps were slow and steady, as if the walker knew exactly where she was going. Step, step, step . . . right toward the cave.

There's no door, Jane thought. And without a door, she

could see that a light was coming toward them as well. It was swinging back and forth in slow arcs. A flashlight!

Step, step, step. Jane didn't dare move. But from the corner of her eye, she saw that the light was being trained on the cave.

In a few seconds the guard would find them.

Jane closed her eyes and waited to be caught. She was already imagining how she would try to explain this to Willow and Katherine. Would they be kicked out of the lock-in—and if they were, where could they go? How would she ever explain what happened to her mother?

But now the light was . . . was it moving away? Could it possibly be that the guard hadn't realized where they were hiding?

She must not have. Because now the light was gone, and the footsteps were walking away.

Still motionless, Jane glanced at the other girls. She could see that they were listening too. A few seconds more, and the sound of the steps was almost gone. Lucy clasped her hands over her head in a silent cheer.

"Wait," Daria whispered. But she didn't need to warn them. The girls weren't going to move until they were absolutely sure the coast was clear.

In her head Jane counted to a hundred. Then two hundred. There was still no sound outside their cramped little hiding place. She looked questioningly at the other girls. "Okay?" she whispered.

"I guess so," Lucy said.

They'd been sitting without moving for so long that Jane had to shake the kinks out of her arms and legs when she could finally stand again.

"That was too much," she told Lucy and Daria crossly. "Being caught by a guard would be even worse than being caught by a mummy. I didn't make this bet— you two did. I'll hunt with you for a half an hour more, and then I'm going back to the Great Hall. By myself, if I have to."

"I guess you're right." Lucy sounded subdued. Then her face brightened. "What about the Hall of Extreme Weather? If I were a mummy, *I'd* want to go to the Hall of Extreme Weather. But wait—we have to get Daria's arm fixed up."

"No need." Daria showed them her arm. To the astonishment of Jane and Lucy, it looked fine. There were no marks on her skin to show what had happened. Her arm seemed to be completely healed.

"How could that happen?" asked Jane. "Your arm was all shredded up!"

Daria shrugged. "I heal quickly."

"Get me off this thing! Get me off!" Jane whispered. Her mouth was dry with fear. But there was no one to help. And she was buckled in. She, Lucy, and Daria were going to have to suffer through the whole tornado before their seats unlocked and they could return to normal.

The Templeton Museum's Hall of Extreme Weather was completely interactive. That made it a lot more interesting than just looking at pictures of different kinds of clouds. Even Daria seemed to loosen up a little. But most of the exhibits were some kind of scary ride, and Jane's stomach was starting to feel woozy. Already the girls had buckled on electronic skis to see how it would feel to be swept up by an avalanche. They'd stood in little booths that felt as hot as the Sahara Desert and as cold as Antarctica. They'd felt the floor shake beneath them in the earthquake simulator and been buried up to their shoulders in fake quicksand. They'd even been struck by lightning—not real lightning, of course, but just as loud and bright.

The tornado simulator was way too realistic for Jane. To ride it, you buckled yourself into a seat and whirled into the air. Or at least that was how it felt. The girls were actually sitting still—only the view in front of them and the vibrations in the floor were changing—but the images on the screen were moving so fast that they were completely believable. The sound of the wind (actually coming from speakers) was so loud it made Jane dizzy. Luckily, no guard would be able to overhear it. The simulator—like all the other rides—was inside a soundproof booth. Lucy explained that this way the museum could still give tours when the rides were being operated.

But Jane wasn't sure what a guard would hear if she suddenly started screaming for help.

Far below, or so it seemed, the girls could see the Missouri farmhouse where the "tornado" had touched down. Now they were moving toward it at terrifying speed. As the ground rushed up at them, Jane closed her eyes . . .

And then everything was quiet. The floor stopped shaking. The ride was over.

With trembling hands, Jane unbuckled her seat belt.

"That was great. Now let's go try One Fateful Day in Pompeii!" said Lucy.

"What happened in Pompeii?" asked Daria.

"You'll see," replied Lucy.

"You two can go," said Jane. Her legs didn't feel too steady. "I'll wait for you. Is there a Hall of *Nice* Weather anywhere around here?"

Lucy laughed. "I don't think so. Just go hang out in Colonial American Life—that's next door. We'll meet you there in a few minutes."

Jane sighed with relief as she headed toward the Extreme Weather exit. When you'd been buried in quicksand and struck by lightning, Colonial American Life would make a nice change.

The colonial galleries turned out to be very, very traditional, which was very, very soothing. Jane wandered happily through an exhibit about candle making and then turned her attention to a wall of samplers. Two hundred years ago, little girls had practiced their needlework by learning to make these samplers. They had cross-stitched wobbling alphabets or little pictures of chicks and flowers. One ambitious girl named Felicity Barrow had tried to stitch a picture of her baby sister. The baby's head was shaped like a mushroom, but Jane—who had never even held a needle—thought Felicity deserved credit for trying.

This is nice, Jane thought. It seemed so peaceful to think of girls her age working calmly away at their sewing.

Then she saw the sampler in the next case.

No pretty flowers here. This girl had stitched a tombstone, and she was much more talented at needlework than poor Felicity Barrow.

It was a very detailed tombstone, in different shades of gray thread. And on it Jane read these words:

Sacred to the memory of my classmate and friend

Jerusha Partridge,

who died **May 19, 1791** in the 12th year of her age.

Come hither, mortals, cast an eye

Then go thy way–prepare to die.

Think on thy doom, for yet thou must

One day, like me, be turned to dust.

Here rests my frame in this cold ground,

Where all of you may soon be found.

Death suddenly took hold of me,

And so the case of you may be.

Death gave to me a sudden call,

I have obeyed and so must all.

Death is a debt to Nature due

Which I have paid—and so must you.

Jane shivered. It was creepy to think of the death of a girl about her own age—and what kind of person put a tombstone on a sampler?

She turned, startled, when Lucy tapped her on the shoulder. "Oh! It's you!" Lucy and Daria were standing right behind her.

"Who did you think it would be?" asked Lucy.

Jane didn't answer her.

"Oh, right," Lucy answered her own question. "The mummy. Well, it's just us."

"What are you so interested in, anyway?" asked Daria.

Jane gestured to the sampler.

"That's so sad!" said Lucy when she'd read it. But Daria was frowning.

"Whoever wrote that poem should have made it shorter," she said. "It just keeps saying the same thing over and over."

"That's true," Jane admitted. "Maybe she just liked to embroider letters. But it's still sad."

"Oh well, it was a long time ago. Let's not think about it anymore," said Lucy. "Pompeii was *great*. We got away from the lava just in time. Let's go see the dioramas."

The dioramas in the next gallery showed what family life in that area had been like two hundred years before. Life-size figures in old-fashioned clothes were posed in all kinds of settings. Daria wasn't much interested, but Lucy and Jane pored over each new scene. In one, a girl untangled wool while her sister churned butter; in another, a man was tapping a maple tree for sap. A string of boys played crack-the-whip on a frozen pond, and a teacher who looked about their age was teaching in a one-room schoolhouse with six students. Pigs strolled through a diorama that showed what the center of town had looked like. It turned out that pigs in the street had been very common back then.

Lucy's favorite diorama featured a blacksmith shoeing a horse. Jane's was a colonial kitchen where a woman was stirring an iron pot hanging on a fireplace hook. The kitchen looked smoky and dark but also cozy. Strings of onions and dried herbs were hanging on the wall, and in the corner a small black cat was dozing next to a baby's cradle.

As the girls were passing on to the next diorama—an old-fashioned barber shop—Lucy came to an abrupt stop.

"Wait a sec," she said. "I saw something moving in the kitchen. Maybe it was the mummy!"

"Don't be ridiculous," said Daria. "A mummy wouldn't go in there."

"How do you know?" asked Jane.

"Look!" Lucy yelled before Daria could answer. Lucy's eyes were wide and scared. She pointed behind the two other girls with a shaking hand.

Jane and Daria turned around.

And stood motionless.

The little black cat that had been dozing in front of the fire was standing up now, its green eyes blazing. As they watched, it stretched for a long second . . . and then slowly began to walk directly toward them.

"This is not possible," said Jane. If she could have screamed, she would have.

The black cat gave a slow blink. Was it Jane's imagination—or was he staring at Daria?

He certainly wasn't scared of her. As they watched, he crossed lazily under the velvet rope and brushed against Daria's ankle. With a little meow, he curled up next to her feet.

"Shoo! Go back where you belong!" Daria shoved the cat with her foot, but he wouldn't budge. He only looked up as if to ask her what was next.

"He must belong to the museum." Jane sounded as if she didn't quite believe her own words.

"Do museums even have cats?" said Lucy doubtfully. "Like, to catch mice and rats?"

Mice, rats, *and* mummies? And not to mention the bugs in the bug exhibit. Templeton Museum was starting to sound *jammed* with things Jane didn't want to meet.

Daria leaned over and patted the cat on the head. Purring, he pressed his forehead up against her hand.

"Don't cats have some kind of sixth sense? Kitty, where do you think we should go next to find the mummy?" asked Lucy.

As if he had understood her, the cat stood up and began to walk away, looking back over his shoulder at them.

"Prrrrrrt?" he meowed encouragingly.

It was too tempting to resist. The girls followed the cat out of the room.

Silently he crossed the wide marble landing that led to the stairs. He padded down the steps, glancing back at them every couple of seconds.

The three girls tiptoed down after him.

On the second floor, he walked leisurely down a row of glass cases holding old pottery beads. He turned left at the installation about frogs and sauntered past a room full of models of sea creatures. Then he paused. Tail twitching, he stared attentively at a niche in the wall. In the niche stood a massive carved totem pole. For some reason a long cloth cord was lying on the floor in front of it. One end of the string was hidden behind the pole.

The cat seemed to be deciding what to do next. Finally he took a deliberate step toward the totem pole.

"What does he want us to do?" asked Jane. "We can see perfectly well from here."

"He doesn't want anything," said Daria. "Let's go. This is—"

The cord on the floor twitched.

The three girls froze.

It twitched again. The cat was watching it closely. He

stretched out a paw and gave the cord a pat. The cord began to move toward the totem pole as if—

As if someone was pulling it in.

The cat was mesmerized, and so were the girls.

"Prrrrrowp?" said the cat. It sounded like a question. As the cord began to vanish behind the totem pole, the cat followed it.

And out from behind the totem pole emerged a pale hand.

CHAPTER 7

The three girls stared.

The hand beckoned the cat invitingly.

"Don't," whispered Jane.

The hand was still beckoning. Now it reached out a little farther. The girls could see a pale, skinny arm emerging from behind the totem pole.

"A skeleton!" exclaimed Lucy.

The hand beckoned again. Silently the cat walked closer. Now he was almost within reach of the hand. And then he was there.

He slid his head under the pale fingers as if he wanted the hand to pat him. He curved his neck and pushed his head upward.

The hand stroked his head gently.

But as he came closer, it made a quick grab and grasped him by the scruff of his neck.

"MrrrrggggOWWW!" the cat yowled. In a split second he had twisted himself free, streaked past the girls, and vanished from sight.

The girls hardly noticed that he was gone. They were staring, mesmerized, at the statue. Someone—or something—emerged from behind it.

It was a girl their own age. She paced slowly and steadily toward them, her eyes unseeing and fixed on nothing.

She was certainly acting strange, but she wasn't a mummy.

"*Megan!*" gasped Lucy. "What are you doing here?"

Megan didn't answer.

She just kept walking. She would have passed them without stopping if Jane hadn't reached out and touched her arm.

"Jane," said Megan in a dead-sounding voice.

"She's sleepwalking!" whispered Jane. "What should we do?"

"I think I read online that you're not supposed to

wake someone who's sleepwalking," said Lucy.

"Fine," snapped Daria. "Leave her here and let's keep looking for the mummy. She'll find her way back to the Great Hall sooner or later."

"We *can't* leave her," said Lucy. "What if she bangs into something and sets off an alarm? She'll die of embarrassment or fright."

"Well, we can't bring her back. Someone else might wake up, and then how would we explain everything?" asked Daria.

Lucy bit her lip, thinking. "You're right. We'll have to wake her up." Gently she shook Megan's shoulder. "Megan? Megan? You need to wake up."

Megan blinked and shook her head a few times. "Hi, guys," she said. Then suddenly she seemed to realize that she wasn't in bed. "Lucy! What are you doing here? Wait, what am *I* doing here?"

"That's exactly what I was going to ask you," said Lucy. "Why were you hiding behind that totem pole?"

"Totem pole?" repeated Megan. "What on Earth are you talking about?"

Lucy pointed, and Megan made a face. "Ewww! I was *totally* not hiding behind that dusty thing!" Then she frowned, thinking. "But I did have a dream that I was hiding behind a tree. I was trying to signal someone, or something."

"Was it a cat, by any chance?" asked Jane.

"Y-y-y-yes, I think so. Yes, that's what it was. I dreamed a cat was lost and I was following it, and it ran up this huge, huge tree. I knew I had to try to coax it down without scaring it. It came closer and closer, and—and then I don't remember what happened. I woke up and I was here."

"Megan, do you sleepwalk a lot?" said Lucy.

"Sometimes, if I get nervous."

"So what you're saying is, you sleepwalk all the time," put in Daria sourly.

"No, no," said Megan. "But I did once wake up in bed with my parka on the night before a test. I must have put it on in my sleep. And once I started playing the piano at three in the morning the day before I had a piano recital. So I guess I must have been nervous about this lock-in or something. I'm so lucky that you guys found me!"

Suddenly she frowned in a puzzled way. "But *how* did you find me? What are you doing here, anyway?"

"We were, uh . . ." Jane's voice trailed off.

"We had to . . . ," Lucy said at the same time.

"We have an errand to attend to," finished Daria crisply. "It has nothing to do with you. So you might as well go back to the Great Hall. And don't tell anyone you saw us!"

Megan looked horrified. "Go back by myself? I'm not walking through this museum alone!"

"Why not?" said Daria. "Nothing happened to you when you were sleepwalking alone."

"But now that I'm awake, I'll be afraid something might happen!" Megan looked pleadingly at Lucy.

"I could walk her back," Jane offered, trying to seize the opportunity to end this little adventure.

"No," said Daria, simply. "The three of us are in this together."

Jane was too tired to protest.

"Please let me come with you on your errand. I can help!" Megan whined.

"I don't think that would be a good idea. You wouldn't like it, I promise," said Lucy.

Megan crossed her arms defiantly. "Well, *I* promise *you* that if you don't tell me, I'll start screaming right now. And I'm really good at screaming. Do you want to hear me?"

She stretched her mouth open and drew in a big breath.

"Fine," said Jane. "You can come with us. It's okay."

Still holding her mouth wide open, Megan made a questioning sound in her throat.

"But you have to promise you won't scream if you come with us," Jane added.

Megan snapped her mouth shut. "I promise," she said.

"Wait," Jane said. "Let us tell you what we're doing before you decide. If you end up not wanting to come, you can walk back to the Great Hall. But either way, you *can't tell anyone* about this."

Megan nodded, and the three other girls quickly filled her in. The argument about the mummy at dinner. The bet. The search so far. Being chased by the guard. Seeing the cat that led them to her.

When they'd finished, Megan said—pretty calmly, for her—"If you think I'm going back to the Great Hall alone to wait for a mummy to come in and shred me with its hook, you're crazy."

"Um, Megan? It's pirates who have hooks," Lucy corrected her.

"Whatever. If a mummy rips me to shreds with its hook, my parents will sue the museum. I'm just saying. I'll go back to the Great Hall, but not without you guys. You have to come with me."

"You know, maybe we should give up anyway," said Lucy slowly. "Even if the mummy's out there, it's not standing there waiting for us to find it. It's probably moving around too. And the museum's way too big for us to search the whole thing." She turned to Daria. "Let's just say you're right. There's no mummy."

Daria looked very smug. "You sure wasted a lot of time figuring that out."

"It wasn't a waste of time," Lucy protested. "We had fun. Didn't we, Jane?"

"I guess we did," replied Jane. She was surprised to realize that it was true.

And she was happy that this ordeal would soon all be over.

"Now all we have to do is find our way back," said Daria.

"I knew we'd get lost," fretted Megan a few minutes later. "Remember how Willow said this place is like a maze? We could be trapped here for weeks! Don't you think we should scream until a guard finds us?"

"No, no! Terrible idea. Look, there's a sign for the Egyptian wing," said Lucy. "We can retrace our steps to the Great Hall from there."

"Doesn't it seem like days since we were last here?" said Jane as they passed through the entrance to the Egyptian exhibit.

"More like years. *Centuries.*" Lucy yawned with all of her body. She felt so tired, she could have fallen over right there, but instead she put a hand out to steady herself against the wall. Except Lucy's hand didn't stop at the wall—it went right through—and Lucy almost fell over for real.

"What?" Lucy said to no one in particular.

"What is it?" asked Jane.

Lucy studied the dusty, dark curtain that her hand was gripping. Its color blended perfectly with the paint color of the wall, but even so, Lucy couldn't believe that for all her times in this museum, she'd never noticed it before. She pulled it back to reveal a small hallway.

"Hold on," she told the other girls. "What's in here?"

"Lucy, let's just go," said Daria impatiently.

"One second," Lucy whispered back.

She peeked her head in and then began to walk through. Right now, it was pretty dark, with only the museum's nighttime lights illuminating the displays. It was more of the same stuff she was so used to seeing in the Egyptian wing. Inscribed jewelry, marble jars, and stone statues. Why these were hidden, Lucy had no idea.

And that's when Lucy noticed it. At first she thought her eyes were playing tricks on her, but there it was in front of her, as plain as day.

"Jane, Megan, Daria," she whispered. Her voice was barely audible.

The other three girls joined her in the corridor and Lucy pointed ahead.

At the end of the small hallway stood a sarcophagus only a little taller than the four girls. Its painted face should have been staring back at them. But it wasn't. Instead the massive stone lid of this sarcophagus had been moved and pushed open. It must have weighed hundreds of pounds.

And with the lid off, the girls could see that there was nothing at all inside the sarcophagus.

Megan had been peeking fearfully over Jane's shoulder. When she finally spoke, she sounded stunned.

"It's empty! Jane, you were—you were right after all."

Her voice was rising to a scream.

"A mummy *is* loose in this museum!"

CHAPTER 8

"Shut up, Megan!" hissed Jane, Lucy, and Daria in unison.

"The last thing we want to do is attract another guard's attention," Jane said.

"But the mummy climbed out! It could be anywhere!" whimpered Megan.

"It did *not* climb out," Daria said emphatically. "Don't be dumb. There are all kinds of reasons a sarcophagus might be open."

"Like *what*?" said Megan.

"Well—for cleaning," said Daria after a second. "Even a sarcophagus probably has to get cleaned once in a while. And look!" She pointed to a dark square on the wall. "All these sarcophagi should have information plaques. But you can see that this one's card is missing."

"That doesn't prove anything about the sarcophagus." Megan sounded sulky.

"Of course it does. It proves they're changing something or moving something or—well—doing *something* with this exhibit. Or maybe there was never any mummy in this sarcophagus. Maybe some grave robber stole it centuries ago. Maybe the museum didn't bother putting a plaque up because this one is just for decoration. Think about it."

"Well, I don't care. I hate this place. Let's get back to the Great Hall. We go out that way." Megan pointed at a distant exit sign. And for once, all four girls agreed on something, and they followed Megan out of the exhibit.

"Before we go back, can we eat something?" asked Lucy a few minutes later. "I'm starving. Do you think the restaurant where we had dinner is still open?"

"Now that you mention it, I'm hungry too," said Jane.

"*I'm* too upset to eat *anything*," said Megan, dramatically. "But maybe my appetite will pick up when we're out of this exhibit. It would probably be good for me to have a snack."

There was no chance of getting lost on the way to the

restaurant—it was right off the main lobby. But the girls walked in silence. They were all tired. Even with their discovery of the open sarcophagus, they hadn't actually *seen* anything and were all weary from the night's adventure.

Unfortunately the museum restaurant wasn't going to solve any problems for them. A big security grate had been pulled across the entrance.

Jane sighed as they headed back to the lobby. "Why didn't I eat more at dinner?"

"I think there's a vending machine in the basement, next to the bathrooms," said Lucy. "Which reminds me that—"

"Which reminds *me* that we don't have any money," said Jane.

"People can't starve to death in a few hours, can they?" said Megan anxiously. "Because suddenly I'm starting to feel faint."

She tottered over to the fountain in the center of the lobby. It had been turned off for the night. Megan plunked herself down on its edge in a swooning kind of way. Then she dipped the tips of her fingers in the water and patted her face dramatically.

"That's a *little* better," she said in a weak voice as she dipped her hand again.

"I guess it's too late to tell her how germy the water probably is," Lucy murmured to Jane.

Abruptly, Megan sat up straight. "Hey, look! There are a lot of coins at the bottom of this fountain! Couldn't we borrow a few for the vending machine? We could pay the money back tomorrow. I, for one, *swear* I will."

"Yes! Great idea, Megan," said Lucy. "Everyone try to get quarters."

Splashing their hands in the cool water revived the girls, and sharing an activity cheered them up. Besides, there were tons of quarters on the pool's tiled floor.

"Eight quarters each ought to be enough," said Lucy. "This is fun! It's like panning for gold."

"Or harvesting pearls," Jane agreed happily.

When they'd collected enough change, the girls headed down to the basement. Five gleaming vending machines were waiting for them at the bottom of the staircase. The machines must have been freshly stocked—they were jammed with candy, drinks, and snacks.

"Thank goodness they have peanuts," said Megan, "because I definitely need some protein."

"What's a peanut butter cup?" asked Jane as she stared at the candy display.

"You don't know what a *peanut butter cup* is? That's like not knowing what a shoe is!" said Megan.

"My mom never has any candy," said Jane. "Are they worth getting?"

Lucy and Megan assured her that they were.

"What are you going to get, Daria?" asked Lucy. But Daria didn't answer. In fact, she wasn't with the three girls anymore.

"I think she's in the" —Megan paused before mouthing the last word—"*bathroom.*"

Lucy slid down the wall to sit on the floor. She opened her candy bar and took a bite. "We can eat while we wait for her."

But when they'd finished their snacks, Daria still hadn't come out of the bathroom.

"I don't want to bother her," said Lucy. "She might be, you know, busy. But maybe I'd better go in there and make sure she's all right."

Megan swallowed her last handful of peanuts and nodded. "Good idea. She may have passed out from hunger in there. It happens to people."

Lucy headed into the bathroom—and almost immediately came out again. "Daria's not in there," she said in a puzzled voice.

"Are you sure?" asked Jane.

"Yes, of course. There are only three stalls in there, and she's not in any of them."

"Is there a window?" asked Megan. "Maybe she felt so faint from hunger that she opened the window to get some fresh air."

"And then did what?" asked Lucy. "Climbed out the window to get even *fresher* air? Anyway, there isn't a window. We're in the basement, remember?"

"I'm trying to remember if Daria even came downstairs with us," said Jane thoughtfully. "She said she was hungry. But did either of you notice whether she actually came down to the basement?"

Silence.

"I don't think she did," said Lucy finally. "She walked to the stairs with us. I do know that. But when we got to the vending machines, I was only thinking about what to buy."

"We all were," said Megan. "All that time, Daria was in trouble. And we never once thought of helping her."

"Wait—why do you say she was in trouble?" asked Jane.

Megan looked at her, amazed. "How could she not be in trouble if she's not with us? She would never leave us on purpose. We're her friends!"

"I wouldn't say that," Jane answered. "I don't think she likes any of us that much. She's been pretty awful since the moment we met her."

"Totally awful," Lucy agreed. "I'm sure there's nothing the matter."

Megan's eyes were wide. "But we still have to find her, right?"

"I guess we do," said Lucy without enthusiasm. "I'd rather just go back to sleep. But it's probably not a great idea for her to be on her own. Anyway, we're wandering around the museum because of her. If we get caught or something, she should be with us to get in trouble too."

That seemed like confused reasoning to Jane. After all, the real reason they were wandering around the museum was that Lucy hadn't been able to resist Daria's dare. But Jane didn't point that out. Instead she asked, "What time is it?" as the three girls wearily began to climb the stairs to the first floor.

"I'm not sure. Probably about two thirty," Lucy replied.

Megan sighed. "This is terrible. I'm supposed to get eight hours of sleep a night."

"*Everyone's* supposed to get eight hours of sleep a night, not just you," snapped Lucy.

"But I always get sick when I get overtired!" Megan said.

"You'll survive," Jane told her. "Now, does anyone have a clue where Daria might've gone?"

"My mom says I always pick the wrong direction," Lucy answered. "I would probably walk straight ahead now. So if I'm always wrong, straight ahead would be the wrong direction. So let's go the opposite way."

Megan looked confused. "You mean, walk backward?"

"No, silly. I mean turn around." Lucy did just that, and so did Jane and Megan. Then Lucy said, "Since the first place I would look *now* is in the Exhibit of Asian Mammals"—she pointed to their left—"we should probably go into the Portrait Gallery." That was on their right.

"Why does a natural history museum have a portrait gallery, do you think?" asked Megan. "Paintings are supposed to be in art museums, aren't they?"

"These are all portraits that Mrs. Templeton owned," Lucy explained. "She wanted them exhibited here, and she was the one in charge, so here they are."

"At least portraits won't be creepy," said Megan.

But Jane wasn't so sure of that once they were inside the first room of paintings. All those shadowy pictures of long-ago people seemed to crowd in on her. She couldn't escape the weird feeling that the people in the portraits were mad at her for being . . . what? Out in the open?

Lucy seemed to share Jane's mood. "See that man in the gold frame?" she said in a low voice. "I think he's watching me. I know people always say that about portraits, but I *swear* I just saw his eyes move."

"I was thinking the same thing about that old lady over there—the one holding the bouquet," said Megan. "When we first came in, I thought she was smiling. But then she frowned for a second. She really did!"

For once, Jane didn't think Megan was imagining things. The room was getting to her, too. It wasn't only the people in the paintings, either. She was sure she'd been in this room before. It was just a feeling, not a memory—but Jane couldn't shake it.

"There's one good thing about this room," Jane said.

"We can see for sure that Daria's not here. There's no place she could be hiding." She sighed. "We'll have to look somewhere else. Lucy, you've been here a lot. Do you have any idea what kind of exhibits Daria would like?"

"She's kind of mean," said Lucy. "If this museum had a torture chamber, I'm sure she'd love it. But it doesn't. Maybe she went to the costume exhibit."

"Fine," said Jane.

The moods of the three girls did not improve when they got lost taking a "shortcut" that Lucy suggested. Instead of leading them to the Costume Hall, her route led them to the Hall of Rocks and Minerals.

"We could check out that baseball-size pearl while we're here," said Lucy hopefully. "Also, they have a magnet thing where you can stick to the ceiling."

"I don't think so," said Jane.

"Me either," said Megan.

As the girls trudged along, Jane gradually became aware of a noise that didn't belong. It was soft, almost gentle—a scraping or brushing, or maybe someone dragging something.

I must really be tired, she thought. *I'm starting to imagine things.*

But why would her imagination dream up such a boring sound?

Whshhhh . . . whshhh . . .

Almost like a shuffling sort of step . . .

"What's that noise?" Megan asked. "That—that brushing sound."

"I hear it too," said Lucy. "I thought I was imagining things."

"That's what I thought too," said Jane. "But if we all hear it . . ."

Whshhh . . . whshhh . . . whshhh . . .

It seemed to be coming from close by, but Jane couldn't tell exactly where. It was much, much worse to know that she wasn't imagining it.

"Do you think someone is sweeping the floor?" asked Lucy quietly.

"Maybe," Megan answered equally quietly. "Maybe the cleaning crew works late. Like really late. But whatever it is, we've got to get out of here before they find us."

"Okay," said Lucy. "Don't run, Megan. Just walk fast. Running would be too loud."

The sound was louder now, closer. It was terrible

not knowing where it was coming from—and not being able to run away from it. Jane had to press down on her thighs to keep from dashing away. But where could they escape to?

Now they were coming toward the end of the hall, which branched off in two directions. "Which way?" Megan whispered.

"Left. No, wait! I'm always wrong! Go *right!*" said Lucy.

Try as she might, Jane couldn't slow herself down. In fact, she was walking faster and faster. So were Lucy and Megan. Hearts pounding, they rounded the corner . . .

And ran smack into the mummy.

CHAPTER 9

A shredded, festering mummy. Its face hidden, its arms outstretched, its bandages dragging on the floor behind it.

No one remembered Lucy's warning about walking, not running. All three girls wheeled around and raced back the way they had come.

"Oh no oh no oh no oh no." Megan was half sobbing next to Jane. Jane wanted to tell her to save her breath, but she couldn't waste her own breath on talking.

She looked quickly back over her shoulder and shuddered. The mummy was running too—a stiff-legged, awkward run like something straight out of a bad horror movie.

But something seemed a little off. As frightened as she was, Jane couldn't help remembering the trick with the fly mask that Lucy had played on her earlier that evening. Still, it wouldn't make sense to stop running. To give up on hope.

These thoughts all flashed through Jane's mind in an instant. Her legs were still pounding along. From behind her, she could hear the mummy lurching closer. And then, out of the blue, it started laughing.

Laughing in a voice that all three of the girls recognized. The mummy raised one hand and ripped the toilet paper off its face, revealing a grinning Daria.

"Gotcha," she said.

Gasping, the three girls stared at her. Then Megan slumped over, panting dramatically. "You almost gave me a heart attack!" she said.

"I knew *you'd* be afraid," Daria answered smugly. "But Jane and Lucy should have seen their faces. They were just as scared as you."

Jane *had* been scared, but now she was furious at herself for having been tricked so easily. She was even angrier at Daria. What a waste of time this whole night had been!

"Hardy-har-har," said Lucy, who also looked very angry. "You know what, Daria? I don't care if there is a mummy in the museum. I'm going to go back to the Great Hall and forget this whole stupid thing."

"It was just a joke!" said Daria.

"A stupid one," Jane replied.

"Well, aren't *we* sensitive?" said Daria sarcastically.

"Please don't fight," quavered Megan. "I get scared when people get mad at each other."

Which was probably the first and last time Jane, Lucy, and Daria agreed about something: Megan was a total baby.

"Anyway," Megan continued, "I never wanted to be *outside* the Great Hall. If you guys hadn't practically kidnapped me after you woke me up, I'd be safe in my sleeping bag right now."

By now Lucy had a pretty good idea where they were. "If we go up those stairs, I think the Great Hall will be right around the corner," she told them. "Let's go."

Jane and Lucy walked toward the stairs in silence. Megan was next to them, still whimpering a protest under her breath.

"—Not comfortable with disagreements," Jane heard

117

her say. "Wouldn't it be great if we could all try to get along?"

Well, it was way too late for that. Daria was trailing the other girls by about twenty feet, trying to peel off her toilet paper bandages as she walked. She looked kind of uncomfortable.

Maybe she was embarrassed that her joke had fallen so flat.

The girls tramped along for what seemed like blocks, getting more exhausted by the minute. "Stay close to the walls so no guards see us," Lucy warned them at one point.

"Maybe they should see us. They might carry us back," said Jane. She yawned. "I've had it with all of this walking."

But there was the sign for the Great Hall at last. Jane blew out a sigh of relief.

"*Shhhhhhhhhhhhhhhhhhhhhhhhh,*" hissed Megan loudly. "We don't want to wake anyone up."

"*You* shush," snapped Lucy. "Which door did you come out of?"

A look of panic crossed Megan's face. "I don't know! I was sleepwalking, remember?"

· "Come to think of that, which door did *we* use?" asked Jane.

Lucy paused. "Uh, this one, I think. But all we have to do is look around for empty sleeping bags, right? We were definitely near one of the doors, because I had us use a different one. And now I realize how dumb that was, by the way."

"Well, there's no way to figure it out while we're standing here. And it'll have to be every girl for herself when we're in there," said Jane. "Just don't step on any sleeping bag that has a girl in it. See you in the morning, Megan."

Megan looked as if she was about to protest, but Jane and Lucy walked quickly into the Great Hall before she could say anything. After a second she followed, with Daria right behind her.

It was so dark that Jane had to stand still for a minute or so until her eyes got used to it. Megan found her sleeping bag immediately and flashed Jane a big thumbs-up. *Good night,* she mouthed silently.

So Megan was taken care of. *Now, what about me?* thought Jane as she tried to remember where Megan had slept in relation to Lucy, Daria, and herself. She was pretty sure that Megan had been across the room from them, which meant that she'd been near the door they snuck out of—which also meant that once again they were going to have to get all the way across the room without waking anyone up.

Every girl for herself. Jane set her teeth and started tiptoeing toward her sleeping bag.

This time, at least, she and Lucy were lucky. None of the other girls woke up, and they didn't trip over anyone. Daria must have made it back safely as well, but Jane never noticed. She was out cold before she'd finished crawling into her sleeping bag.

She'd been asleep for an hour or so when she felt something gently brush her cheek.

"No, Lucy," she murmured thickly. "No more." She turned over onto her back and tried to nestle her head into her pillow.

But where *was* her pillow?

Jane patted the floor around her sleeping bag. No pillow. And now that she thought about it, the floor was even harder than she'd remembered. Had she slid off her foam mattress? Why were her legs out in the open?

Because, Jane realized, she wasn't wrapped up in her blankets, either.

Startled, she opened her eyes.

And she realized that she was no longer in the Great Hall. She was lying on a high, hard surface in the middle of a room that was stiflingly hot.

Was she on a table? In the hospital, maybe? The dim shapes of people she couldn't quite see were hovering over her. She thought she sensed people bustling around behind them as well.

Was I in some kind of accident? she wondered.

Now a sharp, strange smell wafted in her direction. Jane turned her eyes in the direction it was coming from and saw a row of stone jars lined up nearby. The smell was coming from one of them.

Why would a hospital have stone jars?

Jane struggled to sit up—but her legs and arms were too heavy to move. She tried to lift her head. It felt like a boulder that she couldn't dislodge. She tried to scream—but her mouth wouldn't open. She couldn't make a sound. Other than her eyes, she was completely paralyzed.

Helpless, she stared up at the ceiling of the tent overhead.

Wait, she thought. *A tent?*

Where was she—and how had she gotten here?

Then she heard a deep, hollow voice.

"The body is ready."

"Excellent," someone else answered. "Here is the linen."

Someone began to wrap Jane's feet tightly, using what felt like strips of stiff cloth. Then they began wrapping her legs. She could feel the pressure of the cloth against her skin.

It's too tight! she tried to shout—but she couldn't speak.

They were wrapping her torso. From somewhere behind her, a man began to chant.

"Now she will live for all eternity. Now she will meet the great Osiris, Lord of Silence, son of Geb, husband of Isis."

Other voices joined in the chant. Jane's arms were being crossed over her chest and tied down with more bandages.

"Now she will make her home in the land of the blessed dead."

The chanting grew louder and faster as Jane felt the bandages twist around her neck.

"Now she will make her home in the land of the blessed dead. Now she will make her home in the land of the blessed dead. *Now she will make her home in the land of the blessed dead.*"

Now Jane knew what was happening.

She was being turned into a living mummy.

CHAPTER 10

Jane sat bolt upright in her blankets.

Around her the Great Hall was hushed and cool. Everyone was asleep. Nobody was in danger, and nothing bad was about to happen. Through the windows near the ceiling, she could see the first hints of gray morning light.

"Oh, thank you, thank you," Jane whispered to the air. "It was just a dream."

She was breathing hard, as if she'd been running, and it took a couple of minutes for her pulse to slow down. Just a dream, but it had seemed so real! Was that really what being mummified was like? And if so, had she had a dream—or a vision?

Whatever it had been, she was definitely here right now, and she was safe. Jane lay down and stretched luxuriously, savoring the fact that she was the only one awake in this quiet place.

Or was she? Out of the corner of her eye, she saw Daria beginning to sit up a few sleeping bags over.

"Sorry—did I wake you?" whispered Jane.

Daria didn't look at her. Either she hadn't heard Jane or she was ignoring her.

"Daria, are you okay?"

Daria certainly looked very strange. Not as if she'd had a nightmare—more as if she was in a trance. Slowly, slowly, she sat up. Slowly, slowly, she stood up. As she stood motionless for a second, Jane caught a glimpse of her face.

It was as pale as paper. Daria's dark eyes were glowing, and her mouth was set in a mysterious half smile.

"Daria!" Jane whispered it more urgently this time.

Still Daria didn't seem to hear. She began to move away from Jane, walking so lightly that she almost seemed to float. Stepping over some sleepers and walking around others, she headed toward the nearest doorway.

Jane gave an exasperated sigh. Could Daria possibly

be *another* sleepwalker? Should Jane follow and try to wake her? Get one of the chaperones?

It's not as if she's a friend of mine, Jane reasoned with herself. *She's been obnoxious all night. She's gotten me and Lucy into trouble a couple of times. And I've definitely had enough wandering for one night.*

Maybe Daria was just going to the bathroom. In any case, Jane decided not to let it be her problem.

She watched Daria vanish through the doorway. And then she settled back down to sleep.

"RISE AND SHINE! GOOD MORNING, GIRLS! TIME TO WAKE UP!"

"No, no!" Jane mumbled into her pillow. "I've only been asleep for a minute!"

"WAKE UP!" Katherine screeched again. She flashed the overhead lights on and off and then left them on. She and Willow started clapping their hands and stamping through the Great Hall, tugging some sleeping bags and nudging others.

"It's payback time," Willow said cheerfully as she passed Jane and Lucy. "You kept us up late, and now we're waking you up early. I only wish I had a megaphone. C'mon, girls! Get dressed! Breakfast in fifteen minutes! We've got to have you ready to go before the museum opens for the day."

Groaning, Jane lifted her head. Next to her, Lucy was scrunching up her face in protest.

"That light's tooooo briiiiight," Lucy grumbled. "What *time* is it, anyway?"

Jane glanced at the clock. "Seven a.m."

Megan walked up to them, wide-awake and already cramming her sleeping bag into its stuff sack. "I *knew* I wasn't going to get enough rest on this lock-in," she fretted. "Now I'm going to be tired all weekend! And it's your fault," she added, frowning at Jane and Lucy. "Both of your faults."

"Keep it down," said Lucy. "We don't want Willow or Katherine to hear."

"Oh my gosh, that's right!" said Megan. She looked around quickly. "You don't think they heard me, do you? Should we have some kind of—of cover story ready in case they question us?"

Jane laughed. Now that the weird night was over, she felt carefree and relaxed and ready to enjoy the day. It didn't even matter how tired she was.

"They won't ask us anything if they don't hear us," she pointed out to Megan. "I think we're safe. Let's go eat breakfast."

As the girls dressed and packed up their sleeping bags, blankets, and pillows, Jane suddenly remembered: Daria! Had she come back from her trip to the bathroom or wherever she'd gone? Jane scanned the room, but there was no sign of Daria.

"Your pancakes are getting cold. Let's get a move on, girls," Willow remarked as she passed.

"Willow, where's Daria?" Jane asked. Lucy moved closer to hear the answer.

"Daria?" Willow asked. "Who's that?"

"One of the girls we hung out with last night," replied Lucy. "She has dark hair. Wasn't too friendly. Her stuff was next to ours. But she's nowhere to be found now."

Willow frowned and glanced at the clipboard she was carrying. "What was her last name?"

"I—I don't know," Jane admitted. Lucy shrugged in agreement.

"Maybe you didn't catch her name right," suggested

Willow. "Because no one named Daria signed up for this event. I bet the girl you think is Daria is already at breakfast."

Jane and Lucy glanced at each other. They were very confused, but they didn't have any other option except to see if they could find Daria—or whatever her name was—in the dining hall.

But even though Lucy and Jane paced through the dining hall three times looking for Daria, there was simply no sign of her.

The girls were confused, but not panicking yet. "Does it really matter where Daria is?" asked Lucy. "Don't you think she can take care of herself?"

"I guess so," Jane said unwillingly. "But I'd still like to know what happened to her. Maybe we should check the Egyptian wing?"

Lucy's eyes opened wide. "The Egyptian wing! Why on Earth?"

"Because—because—Lucy, I know this is going to sound strange, but I had a horrible nightmare after we got back to the Great Hall." Quickly Jane described the dream, and the way she'd woken from it to see Daria leaving. "I don't know why," she finished, "but I feel like my dream had something to do with Daria. I can't explain it. And since I dreamed about mummies, we need to look at the mummies. And that means checking out the sarcophaguses—I mean sarcophagi."

"All right," said Lucy. "But let's hurry, before people start to notice that we're missing too."

When the girls got there, the sarcophagi in the middle row of the room were lined up as still and silent as ever. But both Jane and Lucy knew where they needed to go. They found the hidden corridor again, and peered to the end of the hallway. The sarcophagus that had been open last night was now closed shut. They hadn't been able to see the painting on the lid the night before with the way the lid had been angled, but now, even though the painting on the lid's surface was highly stylized, they both thought the same thing: The face kind of looked familiar.

Jane's heart was pounding hard enough to wake the dead as she and Lucy crept toward the end of the hall-way. The night before, the card next to the sarcophagus had been missing. Now she could see that it was back.

When she and Lucy got close enough, they silently read the card together.

"This sarcophagus, found in the Valley of the Kings, contains the mummy of an unknown princess. Her tomb contained few clues about her background. Judging by her size, however, she was probably ten to thirteen years old when she died. A small mummified cat—perhaps a pet—was entombed along with her. The hand hieroglyphic seen in various places on her sarcophagus probably stands for something resembling our modern letter D. It's quite possible that the princess's name started with the D sound."

Daria. It had to be.

"So the rumor was true," Jane said quietly.

Lucy nodded. "A mummy *was* haunting the museum."

A mummy who had pretended to be a mummy to play a trick on them.

"I wonder if she comes out a lot," said Jane. "Maybe she's lonely in there."

Lucy snorted. "She didn't act lonely. She acted snotty."

"Well, if she's a princess, maybe that's the only way she knows how to act," Jane replied. "Maybe she doesn't really know how to make friends."

She stared down at the lid of the sarcophagus. The body of a girl their own age was in there, with only her cat to keep her company. She had been in there for so long.

Good-bye, Daria, Jane thought.

"So, new friend!" said Lucy brightly as the two girls made their way back to the dining hall. "How about some pancakes?"

EPILOGUE

FOUR YEARS LATER

"Please, people. We're representing our school. People, please exit the bus in an orderly fashion."

"Why do teachers always call us 'people'?" Lucy whispered to her friend Cailyn as they stood up to get off the school bus.

"I guess they think it makes us feel more grown-up," said Cailyn. "Doesn't work for me, though."

The girls' high school art teacher, Mr. Flaren, was hovering outside the bus now. He looked as flustered as a hen who's lost a chick.

"This way, please, people," he said. "Right up the steps and in the main entrance."

"How *else* would someone get into the museum?" Cailyn muttered.

Lucy smiled without answering. She knew there were other ways into a museum than just the main entrance.

Not that Lucy remembered the lock-in all that well. She was in high school now, with a lot going on. And she and Jane had never managed to connect after the night in the museum. In all the confusion at pick-up time, Lucy hadn't had a chance to get Jane's e-mail address or phone number. She hadn't even gotten to say good-bye.

Lucy had been sorry about that. She'd liked Jane a lot, and she had the feeling they could have been good friends.

She had also wondered about Daria from time to time. As her memory of the lock-in began to fade, Lucy became more and more sure that Daria hadn't been anything more than a grumpy middle-schooler.

Probably nothing unusual actually happened that night, she told herself now, as she and her art class climbed the broad museum stairs. *It's so easy to remember things wrong. And even to remember things that didn't happen.*

Still, she had never managed to entirely shake the feeling that Daria had been the mummy rumored to roam the halls of Templeton Memorial. A mummy that must have been lonely and bored and just wanted to have some fun with them, so she dared them to go on a hunt in a museum in the middle of the night for something she knew they'd never find.

What did it matter now, though? They were visiting the museum during the day. So were tons of kids from other schools. Any supernatural being would have to be nuts to show itself in front of so many people.

Lucy herself hadn't been back to this particular museum since the night of the lock-in. But she was glad to be back at Templeton where she had spent so much time when she was younger. As the years of high school passed, she was becoming more and more sure that she wanted to work in an art gallery or museum, or maybe even become an artist herself. When her school had offered the kids in Lucy's painting class a chance to take a field trip to the Templeton, Lucy had accepted eagerly.

The lobby hadn't changed at all, Lucy saw. It was bustling with field trips from all over the city. A group of excited preschoolers was being shepherded up the stairs. A fifth-grade teacher was telling her class, "I don't want any snickering when we get to the Greek and Roman statues." And Mr. Flaren was practically hopping up and down, he was so flustered.

"Keep together, people," he kept repeating. "I don't want you to get mixed up and think you're part of another class.

"Now, before we go to the Portrait Gallery, we'll take a brief walk through the Egyptian wing, since I know that's a favorite section for many of you," said Mr. Flaren.

Not mine, thought Lucy.

Ever since the lock-in, Lucy had avoided Egyptian art. Somehow it didn't appeal to her anymore. But as she stared at the half-remembered exhibits, she could feel her interest returning.

There was Prince Amun's sarcophagus, and there were the turquoise beads—still as bright as when they'd been made four thousand years earlier. The onyx statue of Horus, the falcon-headed god of the sky. The shards of pottery that were valuable because they showed such realistic scenes of ordinary Egyptian people doing ordinary things.

And down the hidden hallway was the other sarcophagus—the one Lucy couldn't help but check out.

The one that had been open and empty on the night of the lock-in. The one that had been closed the morning after. The one that possibly housed Daria's mummy.

The sarcophagus was closed now, just as it had been the last time she saw it. The ancient painting on its surface stared blank-faced at the ceiling. The image of the unknown princess looked serene and untouched, as if the princess herself had never felt a single emotion.

Lucy leaned over and stared into those intensely black painted eyes. "Are you in there, Daria?" she whispered.

Of course there was no answer.

With a little sigh, Lucy followed Cailyn and the rest of her classmates out of the exhibit. Mr. Flaren was talking about their next stop—the Portrait Gallery one level below. Now that he wasn't so worried about losing people, he had relaxed into his usual teacher-speak.

"There are several things I want you to keep in mind as you study the paintings," he said. "Look at the eyes first. They'll tell you the most about the subject's personality. What about the sitter's expression? And look for little details that might be clues. What about the clothes? What about jewelry? Is the subject rich or poor? Is there anything that shows what interests the subject might have had? And take notes, because we're going to talk about these in the next class!"

Lucy had always loved portraits. She walked into the gallery so eagerly that she almost banged into the guard at the door.

"No need to rush, miss," said the guard in a friendly voice. "The people in these paintings aren't going anywhere, believe me."

The members of her class began to drift around the first room, but Lucy wanted to be more organized. She decided to start with the closest paintings and work her way around the whole gallery.

It's almost like meeting new people, she thought. *The longer you look at the face, the better you get to know the person.* She decided to make a little game out of reading each painting's title before looking at the picture itself. Then she'd be able to compare her expectation with the actual painting.

Frau Schmidstorf Making Lace.

Lucy envisioned a stern, stout middle-aged woman, but Frau Schmidstorf turned out to be frail and elderly, just examining her lace.

The Honorable Hugh Nettlestone.

Instead of the white-wigged old judge Lucy had imagined, Hugh Nettlestone turned out to be a little boy patting a pet rabbit.

Charles Dickens at His Desk.

Lucy already knew what Dickens looked like. No surprise there!

Madame Isabelle Meunier and Her Daughter Jeanne.

This would be a woman giving her baby a bath, Lucy guessed. But no—the two were outside. The woman had her arm around her daughter, who looked about twelve. She had a shy smile and wavy blond hair.

Wait.

Lucy stopped in her tracks.

Jeanne looked just like Jane, the girl she had met that fateful night so many years ago.

Lucy read the card again. Under the title were the words "Early nineteenth-century watercolor by an anonymous artist. A gift to the museum."

And the year that that gift had been made? The same year as the lock-in.

Jeanne . . . Jane. Jane was the English version of Jeanne. . . .

Lucy suddenly remembered that Jane had said

139

something about how she had *just gotten here,* or *just moved in,* or something similar to that. She remembered that Jane hadn't known her own address. Was that because she didn't actually *have* an address outside of the Templeton Museum? She had seemed so shy and awkward at first. Was that because she had never been around real girls?

She didn't even know what a peanut butter cup was, Lucy thought.

"Look at the eyes," Mr. Flaren had told the class. Lucy knew that the eyes in a portrait often seemed to be following whoever looked at the painting. That was an effect used by lots of artists. It had something to do with the way our brains perceive two-dimensional objects.

But Jeanne Meunier's eyes were *definitely* following Lucy now. It wasn't an effect. Jeanne's eyes had widened at the sight of Lucy—just the way Lucy's eyes must have widened when she saw Jeanne.

So Daria hadn't been the only strange guest at the lock-in that night. Like Daria, Jane too had come to life and wandered through the museum. Lucy wondered if Jane had even known that she was only a character in a painting when she was outside of it. She certainly had acted just like one of the girls. And no one had suspected a thing.

As Lucy stared at the painting in shock, Jane gave her the smallest possible wave—nothing more than the fluttering of a fingertip, really.

Then she winked at Lucy.

And the painting was still again.

DO NOT FEAR—
WE HAVE ANOTHER CREEPY TALE FOR YOU!

HERE'S A SNEAK PEEK AT

You're invited to a

CREEPOVER™

Home, Sweet Haunt

Nora used to have a normal life. It was so normal it was boring. She went to school, did her homework, hung out with her friends, had dinner with her family, and avoided her irritating younger brother.

That was before. Before the fire swept through their apartment and her parents changed into nervous freaks.

The fire was in late August. When the school year started in September, her parents wouldn't let her or Lucas out of the apartment. Seriously. Not even into the hallway.

They wanted to be with Nora and Lucas all the time. Protect them from the world. Nora's parents, who had never been afraid of anything, were suddenly afraid to let their children out of their sight. For weeks after the fire, Nora insisted that "lightning doesn't strike the same place twice," but her parents said she was wrong.

Her mother quit her job to homeschool them. Her father quit his job to stay at home as well. They disconnected the Internet. Never replaced the TV, cell phones, or computers that had melted in the flames. Their furniture was charred and all their clothing smelled like barbecue, no matter how many times they were washed.

Nora wished things would go back to the old kind of boring. She'd never complain again.

"Pssst." Lucas stuck his shaggy brown head into Nora's bedroom. "Whatcha doing?"

It was on Nora's tongue to say *None of your business* and toss Lucas out of her room, but she knew that the fire and everything after had been hard for him, too.

Unfortunately, Lucas had a lot of energy to channel.

It was hard, superhard to be nice, but since she didn't have any one else to hang out with, she tried her best.

Nora had gotten permission to push her bed over by the window. The lock still didn't open, but at least she could look outside. There were a few shops and a park across the street.

"Still staring out the window every morning?" her brother asked.

"And afternoon," Nora said.

"You never give up, do you?"

That wasn't really a question, so Nora didn't reply. It was 7:37. Three more minutes. She didn't want to miss seeing her friends. This was the only way.

A few days after the fire, Nora had tried calling them on the only phone that wasn't destroyed in the fire—the one in her parents' bedroom—but the connection was always bad. Although she could hear them perfectly, they could never hear her. Figuring the heat from the flames had melted the wiring, Nora asked her parents to contact the telephone company. That was around the time they called a "family meeting" to announce that they were both quitting their jobs, staying at home, and letting the less important bills lapse. They could no longer afford phones, Internet, and cable TV.

"I have to try," Nora told Lucas. "Maybe if Hallie and Lindsay finally look up at my window, they will see me and come over. There's no way my friends could have forgotten me already."

Seven thirty-eight. She couldn't be distracted. "You can stay here," she told Lucas, "but no talking."

Lucas said, "Even if they did see you, Mom and Dad would never—"

Nora whipped her head around and shot him an evil look. "Shhhh." She put a finger to her lips.

"Forget about them," Lucas said. "We can have an adventure together today. I found this really great—"

"Quiet!" Nora hissed. "I *have* to pay attention." Just past the park was an apartment building much like Nora's. But that one had been renovated. None of their windows were stuck shut, and all their wiring worked.

Hallie and Lindsay lived in that building. In apartments on the same floor, next door to each other.

Nora had only one minute twenty-three seconds to get their attention. That was how long it took them to leave the building, walk by the park, and turn the corner toward school. Today was the day they'd look up.

Nora could feel it in her bones.

Halloween had always been their favorite holiday. The three of them had celebrated it together every year since kindergarten. There was the annual haunted house at the recreation center and then they'd all go trick-or-treating. The night would end with a sleepover at Hallie's apartment and an all-night scary movie marathon. Tonight was the first time Nora wouldn't be there.

Chatting about costumes and candy would definitely

make Hallie and Lindsay think of her. They'd both tilt their heads and glance at her window.

It was going to happen. Nora was sure. And she'd be there to wave to them.

"I'm just saying," Lucas began again, "when the fire department came, they used the old plans to the apartment building like a map. They left blueprints here. There's a—"

"SHHHH," Nora commanded.

Forty-two seconds. She raised her hand and held it flat against the pane. Nora was ready to start waving.

"Your room used to be a butler's pantry room." Lucas said. "Did you know that? These apartments were built to have servants! The kids never had to do chores." Lucas tried to get her attention as he said, "All your baby animal and band posters cover the original wallpaper."

"Whatever." Nora didn't care. Lucas continued yammering, but Nora stopped listening. She saw the shadows of her friends darken the sidewalk before she saw them in person.

"Hallie Malik!" Nora screamed. She waved both her arms wildly. "Lindsay Sanchez! Up here!"

They didn't tip their heads.

If she listened really closely, Nora could hear *them*

talking about Kyle Murphy, a boy in their school. So why couldn't they hear *her* shouting their names like a maniac?

Nora noticed that Hallie was wearing a costume to school. In fact, as the girls stepped into the sunlight, Nora could see that both girls were wearing the outfits they'd all picked out together back in July. Leggings, jean skirts, and neon-colored lace tank tops. Teased-up hair. They were pop stars. This was so unfair. Nora was supposed to be the third of their trio. She leaned toward the windowpane, screaming "Hey!" and "Hello!" and the girls' names over and over. But they didn't react. "It's Halloween!" Nora shrieked. "Remember?! Remember me?!" In frustration Nora clenched her hands into fists when Lucas suddenly reached out and grabbed both Nora's arms.

"No!" he shouted at her, pulling her arms down. "Don't!"

"I only have a few more seconds." Nora yanked her hands out of his.

"But the glass." Lucas dove on top of Nora. "It's weak!"

He was smaller than she was. Nora easily rolled him off of her and pushed past him. "I'm only going to make a loud noise."

"It'll shatter!" Lucas screamed at the same time Nora yelled, "Get out of my way!"

Nora bolted forward. Peeking out the window, she could see that the girls had already passed the park. Thirteen seconds until they disappeared from sight. This was it. This was her chance.

"No!!!" Lucas screamed, grabbing her around the waist.

Nora pushed him away and gave the glass a huge banging pound with both fists simultaneously.

The banging sound was loud like Nora had hoped. And, just like Lucas said it would, the glass also crumbled into a million little pieces.

Nora did a quick check of her arms. No shards of glass stuck in them. No scratches either.

Nora took advantage of the broken window. "Hallie! Lindsay!" Nora leaned out the empty frame to see them looking up toward her broken bedroom window. Nora finally had their attention. "Happy Halloween!" she called.

Hallie looked at Lindsay, eyes wide. Lindsay glanced at the window, then at Hallie. Her mouth hung open in a perfect O.

Nora raised her hands above her head. "Come over later! Trick-or-treat in my building tonight! I'll ask my parents. I'm sure they'll let me go with—" She lost her balance. "Aghhhhh!" Nora flailed as she fell forward and farther out the window.

Lucas grabbed Nora and pulled her back an instant before she fell ten stories to the pavement.

"No, no, no! Let go of me!" Nora kicked him in the shin and tore out of his arms. She peered out the window frame.

The street was empty. Her friends were gone.

Nora spun on her brother. "Get out of my room. Get out and never come back!"

"I saved your life," Lucas replied.

"They didn't answer me!" Nora screamed. "They won't come over and I'll never convince Mom and Dad to let me go out with them. No candy. No scary stories. Halloween is ruined! It's all your fault!" She threw a pillow off the bed at Lucas's head. He ducked and she missed. By a mile.

Her terrible throw made Lucas laugh. When Nora scooped up a second pillow and tossed it again, he stuck out his tongue before dodging her throw.

"WAR!" Nora declared. She leaped on her brother and wrestled him to the ground.

He was small, but quick. Lucas managed to roll away from Nora, swooping a pillow off the floor as he made his escape. With a wallop, he hit *her* in the side of the head.

"Ooof!" Nora grunted, grabbing the other pillow and

swinging it back at Lucas with all her might.

Direct hit. The seam burst open. Nora dove forward, hitting him over and over again with the torn pillow until feathers were everywhere. Lucas chuckled as he hit her again with his own pillow. That pillow also ripped and more feathers poured into the room. Back and forth they went until the pillowcases were empty. Then they started throwing handfuls of feathers at each other.

"I win!" Nora exclaimed, holding her brother's arms behind his back. "And now you will suffer."

"You did not win! I did!" Lucas giggled. With a shove, he tipped her over and tried to hold her firm. Nora was struggling against his grasp when their mother walked into the room.

"What is going on here?" Nora's mother glanced around before calling, "Frank!" to her husband.

"Laura, I—" Mr. Wilson began as he reached Nora's bedroom. His voice dropped. "Whoa."

Nora and Lucas were wrapped together on the floor, a tangled mess of arms and legs. The room was covered with white feathers. It looked like it had snowed.

The window was broken.

And shattered glass covered Nora's bed.

WANT MORE CREEPINESS?

Then you're in luck, because P. J. Night has
some more scares for you and your friends!

Hidden Code Hieroglyphics

A B C D E F G H I J K L M N

O P Q R S T U V W X Y Z

P. J. Night has created a code using hieroglyphics.
Can you decipher P. J.'s message below?

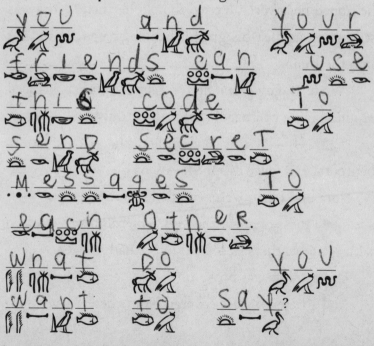

you and your
friends can use
this code to
send secret
messages to
each other.
what do you
want to say?

YOU'RE INVITED TO . . .
CREATE YOUR OWN SCARY STORY!

Do you want to turn your sleepover into a creepover? Telling a spooky story is a great way to set the mood. P. J. Night has written a few sentences to get you started. Fill in the rest of the story and have fun scaring your friends.

You can also collaborate with your friends on this story by taking turns. Have everyone at your sleepover sit in a circle. Pick one person to start. She will add a sentence or two to the story, cover what she wrote with a piece of paper, leaving only the last word or phrase visible, and then pass the story to the next girl. Once everyone has taken a turn, read aloud the scary story you created together!

What do you want to say?

Answer: You and your friends can use this code to send secret messages to each other.

My grandmother's house has always felt like a museum to me. It's filled with treasures, souvenirs, and knickknacks from her adventures all over the world. Most of the stuff is really cool, like a perfectly detailed miniature replica of the Taj Mahal, and rocks formed from the lava of one of the world's most active volcanoes. But there's one thing she brought home that's always bothered me. It seems so ancient and . . . cursed. It's a . . .

_____

_____

_____

_____

_____

_____

_____

_____

_____

_____

_____

THE END

Did you **LOVE** this book?

Want to get access to
great books for **FREE?**

Join

bookloop

where you can

✗ Read great books for FREE! ✗

• Get exclusive excerpts •

§ Chat with your friends ≩

Log on to join now!

∞ everloop.com/loops/in-the-book

A lifelong night owl, **P. J. NIGHT** often works furiously into the wee hours of the morning, writing down spooky tales and dreaming up new stories of the supernatural and otherworldly. Although P. J.'s whereabouts are unknown at this time, we suspect the author lives in a drafty, old mansion where the floorboards creak when no one is there and the flickering candlelight creates shadows that creep along the walls. We truly wish we could tell you more, but we've been sworn to keep P. J.'s identity a secret . . . and it's a secret we will take to our graves!